PRAI

THE RUNAWAY RESTAURANT

"Dream-drenched and sinuous, the stories in Tessa Yang's *The Runaway Restaurant* sing with the weird magic of being alive. Yang conveys both humor and heartache with equal grace—and every glimmering gem of a story reveals another avenue we might take to find ourselves, our shared humanity. This collection is an absolute delight."
—**Allegra Hyde, author of** *Eleutheria*

"Reading *The Runaway Restaurant* is like sifting through a series of exquisite dreams—these stories are shimmering, inventive, and beautifully layered. Tessa Yang is a bold and gifted writer, and this is a stunning debut."
—**Kimberly King Parsons, author of** *Black Light*

"Through cybernetic implants, weather-bending super-powers, and a world-ending plague, Yang deftly illuminates the contours of fractured childhoods, of human alienation and desire. Yang's voice is so assured and compelling that, while reading *The Runaway Restaurant*, I had the rare experience of not wondering if the next story would be good, but assuming it would be. I make the same assumption of her future books. This is a writer to watch."
—**Kim Fu, author of** *Lesser Known Monsters of the 21st Century*

THE RUNAWAY RESTAURANT

by

Tessa Yang

7.13 Books
Brooklyn

Printed in the United States of America

First Edition
1 2 3 4 5 6 7 8 9

Cover art by Alban Fischer
Edited by Leland Cheuk

Library of Congress Cataloging-in-Publication Data

ISBN (paperback): 979-8-9853762-8-9
ISBN (eBook): 979-8-9853762-9-6
LCCN: 2022944596

For Cara and Nick

STORIES

PRINCESS SHIPWRECK

MONSTERS HAVE ABSCONDED WITH the lifeboats. Their fins ruffle the ocean's surface as they wheel and tug those punctured rafts into the depths. On the beach, we're a splayed catastrophe of waterlogged slippers and sand-streaked gowns. Nevertheless, we're polite. *Pardon me, could I perhaps assist you in removing the seaweed from your hair? It seems your tiara's gotten washed away—would you like to wear mine for a while?* During times of stress it's easy to fall back on the old finishing school lessons, the memories of governesses tapping our slouched spines straight.

We set out to explore the island. Sand gives way to forest, which gives way to rock, which rises in a towering black cliff that throws a blade-like shadow over the trees. We're looking for the usual staples: food, fresh water, shade. But being who we are, we're also on a quest for some stray, beautiful thing. Our young lives have been bound up in beauty. We don't know ourselves without it. We comb sand and plunge through caverns and climb to the highest, frailest tree branches, leaving shreds of lace that dangle like flags. When the sun flames at the top of the cliff, we return to the beach, rich in palm fruit and hollow shells that brim with cold creek water. Yet we are ugly and defeated.

Night creeps around the bonfire's circle of light. From the ocean comes the noise of frantic splashing and a fierce, slobbering crunch. Someone begins to weep, and soon we're all weeping. Our tears make gray freckles in the sand. They sprout no blossoms. They summon no fairy godmothers. Princess tears are just tears. Water and salt. We miss our handsome boyfriends. We miss our talking animal friends. We miss feathered mattresses, cobbled courtyards, silver teaspoons, white horses, banquets, mirrors, music, and magic wands.

We cry until we're all dried out. Then someone stands. She tosses an armful of driftwood on the dying fire. Her hair is a dark road running out into the beach.

"I'll tell you what I won't miss," she says. "Those high cold tower rooms where there's nothing to do but stare out the window all day."

The flames pop. Sparks land on our dresses, flare, and fade. The girl stares brazenly at each of us until a hesitant voice offers, "Stepmothers?"

A murmur of assent.

"Definitely won't miss them."

"Seriously unbalanced people."

The long-haired girl nods encouragingly. Someone tosses more sticks onto the fire. It emits a merry roar as it eats through the brittle, salty wood. We hold out our hands and feel the heat against our palms.

"Well, I won't miss all those enchanted comas," says a girl in a filthy yellow dress. "Every time you fall asleep, wondering if it'll be years and years before you wake up."

"My boyfriend sent out a search party whenever I went for a walk."

"My talking birds always interrupted me."

We laugh. We sip creek water from our shells. The long-haired girl stoops and pulls a sand crab out of her tresses. In our old lives, it was the sort of creature that would have repulsed us. Now we admire the black eyes in the radiant blue face, and the delicate white hairs on its jointed limbs.

"Beautiful," someone whispers. The crab flexes its legs. We take it up as a chant. "Beautiful. Beautiful. Beautiful."

The island opens itself to us after that. We revel in its secrets. There are worms with charmed eyes strung from branches like hoop earrings. Sticky purple sap oozes down tree trunks and tastes bittersweet. In the boiling springs of green mud deep within the caverns, glowing dragonflies alight on the greasy bubbles, then flit away when they pop.

With our gowns reduced to tatters, we construct skirts out of twigs and leaves, but the kelp we use for thread slides free from its knots, and soon enough we're naked. Our bellies are bloated from the palm fruit. We play them like drums, slapping out hollow rhythms that echo between trees. Our skin burns and peels. Crabs make off with the dead bits and build miniature castles on the sand. We laugh to see their labors, laugh harder when the tide comes in and drags these fragments of ourselves out to sea. We've forgotten our fears and our sadness. We've taken new names after what we like to do best.

I am Fisher Woman.

I am Fruit Fetcher.

I am Snake Crusher.

The cliff we name Mother, and nestle in her innumerable caves when the wind drives a warm stinging rain up the beach.

It's to Mother we flee when the sailors come searching. Their grins appear clownish in the moonlight. The sails of their ships blaze like white fire. We run, the dragonflies lighting the way, to the shallow strip of beach beneath Mother's shadow. We clutch our fishing spears and snake-crushing rocks. The sailors call out names of flowers and precious stones. We try not to think about their big shoeprints in the sand. They'll be gone soon. They'll leave without ever seeing a single beautiful thing. We crouch in the darkness, timing slow breaths with the tide's rolling. Monsters glide from the water and rest their spiked chins at our feet.

BIOHACK

THE FIRST OF HER mother's models Cami tried to sleep with told her she was too young. He would turn out to be the ugliest, though she didn't know this at the time. She was seventeen, and the sight of those glowing discs pulsing at his human wrists raised a tingle in her thighs. When she reached out to touch one, he closed his hand around hers, gently. "You should go," he said.

Cami wound through the crowd of makeup artists and reflective umbrellas, feeling hideous and jilted. Electronic music throbbed from hidden speakers. Her mother was somewhere, invisible and omnipresent as God. At the threshold, Cami turned and caught the blinding flash of a camera she imagined was for her: a teary yet stunning portrait of first rejection.

The second model was a hottie. Of this, Cami was sure. She met him at an after-party in a hotel banquet room full of chairs that looked like tongues. A white guy, his brown curls long on top and shaved to stubble at the sides, a tasteful line of circuit boards running up his left arm. When he spied Cami watching him over the table of salmon croquettes, he smiled roguishly, like a Disney villain. For him, Cami was not too young. She was shirtless on the bed of a first-floor hotel room before he even asked for her name.

"Camille Morimoto."

"Like—*the* Morimoto?"

"She's my mom." Cami wrapped her legs around the model's waist. A second line of circuit boards peeked over his belt buckle, and she wanted to see how far down they went. He took hold of her ankles, extracted himself from her embrace, and began to rapidly dress.

"Why?" asked Cami. In an effort to correct for the syllable's unintentional whine, she sat and tossed her bangs out of her eyes in what she imagined to be a careless, seductive gesture.

"This may surprise you," said the model, "but I don't actually have any marketable skills. This job is the only thing between me and a lifetime laying turf for my brother's landscaping company. I'm not throwing that away for one fuck."

She vowed never to give her full name again, but it didn't matter. After years of shielding her from the limelight, her mother finally decided Cami was old enough to start attending galas and charity events. *Teen Vogue* printed a story: "A Day in the Life of a Fashion Mogul Princess." Gone was the era of floating anonymously around photo shoots, a pretty and innocuous face readily mistaken for an intern. Makeup artists pressed free samples into her hands. Cybernetic surgeons asked tedious questions about her schoolwork. The models regarded her with a deference she found deeply un-sexy. When her third, fourth, and fifth targets barely made eye contact, Cami did the only thing she knew to do when she wasn't getting her way: She went to her mother to complain.

"Are they disrespecting you?" asked Ivy Morimoto. "Are they mistreating you? Are they harming you in some way?"

"No," Cami admitted.

They were ensconced at the top of Morimoto Mansion in her mother's home office, an attic room with vast skylights showing rectangles of bright September sky. The furniture was sparse and simple. On her own person, Ivy's only extravagance was a number of hammered silver rings adorning her stubby fingers. She disdained hardware on the grounds that it was perverse for a designer to partake in her own designs. She did not cut an impressive figure. Her posture was poor, hair oily, fingernails chewed to raw nubs. A filthy film coated the lenses in her glasses. It annoyed Cami that her mother had never fully shed the skin of the beleaguered nerd she'd been growing up.

"But they're afraid of me," Cami went on. "Because they're afraid of you. Of getting fired. I don't feel like a person around them."

"You could have any boy you wanted, Noodle. So why settle for a model? They're like cattle. They receive their brandings, go where they're told. There must be some boys at school who've caught your eye."

Cami made a noncommittal noise and scraped a fingernail around the embossed initials on her cell phone case. Yes, there were a few handsome boys at her private high school. And yes, as the sons of senators and world-class entrepreneurs, they were sufficiently unimpressed by Cami's pedigree to consider sleeping with and subsequently abandoning her, same as they would any other girl. But the implants remained illegal for minors. The bodies of her classmates were not spangled with the ports, screens, and adapters that Cami dreamt of each night—unless you counted the grinders, that weird clique of unwashed wannabes who ate lunch in the stairwell and stuffed LED lights beneath their skin, and who really did?

Ivy closed the small red notebook where she'd been sketching a new design. "You remember Dr. Felch? The surgeon from Connecticut? He has a son, Andrew. A sophomore at NYU, studying computer science. A very good-looking boy. Should I make the introduction?"

Cami sighed and said yes, fine, whatever. She left her mother's office and went to her bedroom downstairs. The walls and floors were strewn with the detritus of an indecisive mind: magazines opened and abandoned; crumpled posters of bands and TV shows she no longer followed; heaps of tie-dye from her bohemian phase, denim from her cowgirl phase, and leather from her Goth phase. Ivy probably thought this fixation on the models was just that: another craze that would wither like all the rest. She had no idea how far Cami's desires extended. When she looked into her future, she didn't see a career or a family or even a college major, but an endlessly rotating door admitting new lovers, their skins beaded with metal and light.

The sixth model that Cami solicited was a woman. Cami thought she could be forgiven for the error. Her mother's latest brain-wave—that cybernetic fashion transcended the petty labels of sex and gender—had resulted in a surge of tall, androgynous figures drifting around the photo shoots. Cami didn't realize her mistake until after she'd murmured her trusted pickup line about "getting to know each other somewhere private," and the model, smiling, said, "Just name the time and place."

Cami was flustered, but recovered quickly. Implants were implants, and this woman boasted more hardware on her visible skin than Cami had yet seen. The flesh on the left side of her neck had been replaced with ribbed steel sheeting. Blinking bands joined wrists to arms, forearms to elbows, ankles to feet. They traded phone numbers. The woman's name was Lucia Chon—syllables Cami would mouth in the darkness before bed that evening, and every evening for a long time after that. She named the luxury hotel six blocks from her high school. "Friday after-noon. 3:00 p.m."

That week in school, Cami was more distracted than usual. She flunked two quizzes and "umm-ed" her way through a presenta-tion about the Revolutionary War. At the lunch table, where she traditionally reigned over Susan, Zoe, and Ming, she drank her Diet Pepsi and frowned into the distance, as though trying to read a sign hanging from the far wall. When Zoe asked what was the matter, Cami said, "Cramps," and they all nodded wisely.

The truth was, Cami didn't feel very invested in these girls. They'd found each other freshman year and bonded over their shared obsession with a reality television show called *Left at the Altar,* which followed abandoned brides trying to rebuild their romantic lives. After the show was canceled, they found themselves with little to talk about. But the cliques had already been formed and slowly a mutual recognition settled upon them that they were stuck with each other until graduation.

Cami thought of *Left at the Altar* as she waited in the hotel room on Friday. Each episode began with a dramatized retelling of the groom's last-minute desertion: the guests whispering behind their fingers, the woman wailing in her white dress. There was something so gorgeous about the moment's heartbreak. Cami had envisioned herself in that position a hundred times. When she heard the knock on the door, she leapt to her feet as if scalded and realized she had once more allowed her imagination to slot her in the place of forsaken lover: She had not expected the model to show up.

Lucia stepped into the room. The heavy door swung shut behind her. She wore leggings and a graphic T-shirt and a denim jacket that hid all her hardware but the implant on her neck. She sprawled across the bed as if it were her own room and kicked off her combat boots. They landed on the carpeting with twin clunks. "Do you do this often?"

"Yes," lied Cami.

At the photo shoot, Lucia had radiated a pristine stiffness that was perfectly robotic. But here she seemed so warm. So alive. Her dark hair was pleasantly disheveled, as if she'd just stepped in from a breezy balcony. Pale freckles dusted her nose. Cami was intimidated. When Lucia kissed her, she tensed up, forgot all she had learned during those practice sessions with dull boys at middle-school dances. They broke apart. Lucia stared at her, a silent laugh lighting her eyes. Cami felt a fire flaring in her belly: of challenge or desire, she wasn't sure.

They kissed again. Longer this time. Lucia shrugged out of her jacket. With the glee of a treasure hunt, Cami's fingers uncovered more of the gear built into her body: dials lodged between vertebrate, a tiny screen in her sternum, a dime-sized port where a belly button would normally be. These implants were some of her mother's finest, more beautiful for being functionless, as if they existed for pleasure alone. Cami didn't know how to touch them and settled for stroking them with her fingertips, but Lucia encouraged her to be rougher. "They're surgically implanted. They're not gonna fall out." Soon Cami fell inside their joined movements, which she imagined not as the movements of two people but of a vast, networked beast, its invisible feelers crawling across the planet to all the places she'd never been.

When she finally made her way back to the mansion, still wobbly-legged with pleasure, she found the sidewalks clogged with protestors. Judging from their severe haircuts and necklines, they were the Christian kind, "the Bible boys" as Cami's mother called them, though there were women, too, the breeze whipping their hair into furious currents of brown and blonde.

"Spawn of Satan!" one of them cried, pointing at Cami. She held a huge white sign the wind kept trying to carry away. *Corinthians 6:19: Do you not know that your bodies are temples of the Holy Spirit?*

Joel, a scowling, balding white man who handled security for the estate, guided Cami through the mansion's iron gates. On the front step, she turned and blew the hissing protestors a kiss.

"You shouldn't provoke them," warned Joel. "They're more dangerous than they look."

"You're so paranoid," said Cami. She shut the door in his face before he could respond.

Her footfalls echoed as she ascended the staircase to the upper floors. Ivy was off somewhere, meeting with surgeons, reviewing the proof of her winter catalogue. The house would be empty but for Justine, the old nanny-turned-cleaning-lady, and Cami's tutor, Marvin, who'd be running around looking for her while she hid out in the one place he was not allowed to go. Cami entered the security code in the panel outside her mother's office. After years of whining that it was unfair she couldn't access a room in her own house, Ivy had relented and given Cami the code for her fourteenth birthday. Now Cami ventured inside when she needed to do some thinking. Her own room was too chaotic for introspection. She lay down on the rug and looked up as an airplane floated across the skylights, trailing a wisp of blue-gray.

If sex with the model had been so good, why did Cami feel so queasy? The heat that had slipped into her belly when Lucia kissed her now swelled to her fingers and toes. She felt feverish. A goofy, sluggish grin spread across her face. She braced her palms against her stomach to quell its fluttering. When her phone chimed, she thought it might be Lucia, declaring that one week was too long to wait and she must have Cami again right now.

Hey this is Andrew ☺
Who?
Andrew Felch
Who?
Is this Camille Morimoto?
Never heard of her.

He sent a string of apologies and promised to delete the wrong number at once. Cami turned her phone on silent and threw it across the room.

The prospect of those Friday afternoons quickly became her only incentive for rising each morning. Though she soon memorized the bolts and buttons of Lucia's body, their lovemaking retained an element of discovery, slightly different each time. There was nothing relaxing or easy about it. Cami left the hotel feeling restless and inadequate, as if she'd made some critical error and it would be an entire week before she had the chance to correct it. She cringed to hear herself begging Lucia to come back to bed, to stay longer, to share something of her life so that she, Cami, might lay some claim over the person the model became when they weren't together.

Lucia weathered these demands with good humor. "You'll wear me out," she said, laughing and pushing Cami away as she rose to dress. "They'll need to replace my parts. I'm not as young as you are, you know," though she could not have been older than twenty-five. She seemed totally comfortable there in the hotel room. She belched and farted and scratched herself. When she used the bathroom, she left the door wide open—a habit Cami found simultaneously endearing and gross.

After she left, Cami stuck around the hotel room. She stripped the bed and folded the sheets and pillowcases into neat squares. She stood naked before the bathroom mirror, tracing the uneventful contours of her flesh.

"You're in love, aren't you?" asked Ming, unprompted, one day at lunch.

Cami looked up from the magazine in her lap. It was her mother's winter catalogue. The opened page showed a photograph of Lucia. She stood in a fighting stance, fists raised to reveal the metal fasteners gleaming at her wrists. The harsh, clinical lighting sapped her color. Her slicked-back hair glinted bright as a helmet.

"Ew," said Zoe, peering over Cami's shoulder. "Who'd want to go clacking around with all those robot parts?" Then she seemed to remember who she was talking to and added, "I mean, they're super cool and all. Like, *really* well-designed."

"Shut up, Zoe," said Ming. She had always been soft-spoken, but over the past month, as Cami withdrew, she'd risen to become the alpha of their little lunchtime kingdom. Cami felt only slightly annoyed about this. She had higher concerns. "I was asking Cami a question. Now c'mon! Who is it? We won't tell."

Zoe and Susan nodded, ponytails bouncing. Cami considered. "His name is Andrew. He's a sophomore at NYU."

The girls squealed. "A *college* guy?" That set them off on a discussion about the merits of older men.

In fact she had started seeing Andrew Felch. After ignoring several more of his texts and Facebook messages, she'd decided that she could use the diversion. They'd met for coffee and made out on a bench once or twice. Most of the time they just walked around Central Park, complaining about their parents. Dr. Felch was a nervous, bumbling man who had exactly one talent—installing hardware in people's bodies—and faked his way through everything else. Mrs. Felch was a door-slammer and a screamer who'd taken up lovers all over the city, most recently, the physics teacher at Andrew's old prep school, whom Andrew had come upon one afternoon banging around the kitchen, searching for sriracha. Cami talked about her father down in Tampa, flitting from one terrible business investment to another. There wasn't too much to say about Ivy except that she was never around. Conversing with Andrew was easy, and Cami admired his glumness, so different from the high energies of boys her own age. But she knew he was not the one she was in love with.

She returned her attention to the catalogue and stirred the cold mac and cheese around her plate. She found she no longer required much food or sleep. Nights, she motored joyfully through the dark house, a wind-up toy charged on its most recent encounter with Lucia. Sometimes she came upon her mother wandering in her dorky flannel. Ivy's jaw was slack, her eyes half-shut. Cami had thought her mother's sleepwalking terribly frightening as a child. Now she rolled her eyes, took Ivy by the arm, and led her back to her bedroom, chanting under her breath all the while: "I'm fucking your model and there's nothing you can do!"

Though they were well into December and snow crusted the sidewalks, Lucia continued to wear only her denim jacket. Cami watched her get dressed from the bed. They'd kept the thermostat set low. The sheets tucked around her body were pleasantly warm, but a cold fear gnawed behind her breastbone, as it always did at the prospect of Lucia's departure.

"Why are you doing this?"

Lucia shrugged. "The same reasons you are. Boredom. Lust."

Her tone was cheerful, but Cami felt a small wound opening in her chest. This was not the answer she'd wanted. She propped herself on an elbow. "Aren't you worried my mom's gonna take away your hardware if she finds out?"

"She can't. There's a contract. I agree not to sell her designs. In exchange, I get to keep the implants for life. It'd be too danger-ous to remove them all."

"She could still fire you. She could ban you from photo shoots. Ruin your reputation so none of the other designers will want you." Cami didn't know why she was pushing this, except that she had experienced a sudden and confusing desire to make Lucia unhappy.

The model only shrugged again.

"Cyber fashion is on its way out. People don't want tech you can wear. They want tech that can actually do things. Scan your body for disease. Put phone calls right into your brain."

"That sounds like science fiction."

"That's the future," said Lucia. "Ivy Morimoto won't be a big name much longer."

"But the other models before you—they were terrified of getting fired."

"Maybe they couldn't read the terrain like I can." Lucia grinned lazily. "C'mon, Cami. You're not a little kid anymore. You have to know your mom's not invincible. You read the news, don't you?"

Cami didn't. But as soon as she got home, she googled her mother for the first time in years. What she saw made her stomach drop. The top headlines read "Ivy Morimoto: The End of a Regime" and "Cyberwear: Fashion Revolution or Geeky Fad?" It embarrassed Cami that she wasn't only ignorant of these issues: She had never even thought to ask about them.

Ivy had been the face of cyber fashion since Cami was five years old. She remembered the suffocating admiration she used to feel for her mother. How at the sound of the front door opening, she'd race from Justine's side and throw herself around Ivy's legs, eager as a dog and just as willing to forgive her long absences. If someone had claimed her mother designed the moon and the rain, Cami would have believed them.

She could not eat. Her body gleamed and trembled like a blade. At school, she cut herself off from her friends, disgusted by their latest obsession with a reality TV show about near-death experiences. She turned to the grinders in their stairwell. They already knew who she was.

"Your mother is what we call a *mainstreamer*," said their leader, a small boy with staples running up his right forearm like a tiny railroad track. The whole thing looked a little infected. "She's in this for selfish, capitalistic reasons. She's not interested in the next stage of human evolution."

"I'm nothing like my mother," snapped Cami.

After a brief consult, their studded heads bent together over the bottommost step, the grinders agreed to give her a trial run.

The following Saturday, Cami took a taxi to the Brooklyn address the stapled boy had written on her arm. She paid the cover and stepped into a large warehouse strung with naked blue light bulbs. There was no heat, the space warmed only by the crush of bodies swaying and jerking to the music. Some of the partygoers looked like they could've been Ivy's models, their hardware sleek and elegant, metal joined cleanly to flesh. Others had implants the likes of which Cami had never seen: wired skulls and rusted Frankenfingers with freshly puckered scars and mysterious subdermal lumps suggesting buried gadgets. The bartender who passed her a sparkly beverage before Cami even told him what she wanted sported an overlarge dial where his left eye should've been, his whole head listing sideways as if the device were pulling him earthward. It twitched, needles whirring in her direction, as she reached for the glass. Cami longed to ask what it was doing, but didn't want to seem like an awed tourist.

Her classmates were huddled near the back, wearing expressions of purposeful boredom even as their hands quivered around their glasses. Cami copied their slouches. Every few minutes a door would open, sucking in someone from the shortening queue. When it was their group's turn, they all stood around looking at each other until Cami plunked her empty glass on the floor and strutted over the threshold. So she was to be the guinea pig. Fine and good. She'd wear that title with pride.

Her confidence wavered once she was inside the closet-like chamber, a far cry from Dr. Felch's sterile operating suites. A potbellied man with about a thousand facial piercings squatted on a stool near a space heater. He was missing a leg. Cami tried not to look at the stump. His eyes rolled up and down her body.

"Virgin?" he said, smirking.

Cami held his stare. He beckoned to a chair beside the stool and she sat.

"Did you do all those people out there?"

"Some." The surgeon opened Cami's palm with latex-gloved fingers. "I'm part of a team of innovators. We work for free. We're not interested in perpetuating the pleasures of the rich." He looked at her again, and Cami realized he knew exactly who she was.

His voice became a soothing purr as he reached for his platter of tools. "We'll start you off nice and easy . . ." Cami squeezed her eyes shut. The cool damp of an alcohol wipe. A hot sharp pain only partially dulled by the lingering buzz of the sparkly beverage. She nearly bailed when she felt the tiny magnet being forced inside the open wound, but thoughts of Lucia kept her glued to the chair. Then it was over, she was lurching back into the blur of bodies and music, her hand raised in triumph, the grinders gawking at the blood oozing down her wrist. Just like that she was queen again, another group held in her thrall.

What grudging respect she'd maintained for her mother evaporated in the weeks following that slapdash surgery. The warehouse had offered a precious glimpse of something, a shadow world of pioneers who disdained Ivy Morimoto's blessing. Cami gained a vindictive pleasure in berating her mother for her professional decline.

"Cyber fashion isn't over, Noodle," Ivy explained. "It's changing. Those of us who are able to change with it will survive."

"And what about people who can't?" demanded Cami.

Ivy plucked a mushroom from her soup with two fingers and squeezed it as though testing its fragility. It was the first time they'd eaten together since the gloomy Christmas holiday they'd spent in Amsterdam, Ivy smoking joints in the bath, Cami sulking because she had missed two consecutive Fridays with Lucia.

"You're not willing to take risks," pressed Cami. "You've been relying on the same tech for the last four years. And you don't have any implants. It's suspect. Like a chef who won't eat her own food." She was paraphrasing from an article she'd read last night on technoweird.com. "No one cares about your work anymore. No one's excited by it. When's the last time you saw the Bible boys? Even the protestors have forgotten all about you."

The mushroom slipped from Ivy's fingers. It hit the soup with a tiny splash. Cami hadn't thought she was getting to her mother, but she saw Ivy's chewed fingernails curl into her palms and knew she'd gone too far.

"Do you think I'm an idiot?" asked Ivy.

Cami lowered her eyes to her bowl. "No."

"Well, you must," said Ivy, her voice cracking, "to believe I wouldn't notice three months' worth of hotel reservations on my own credit card."

Cami looked up. Falling snow swirled gray shadows against the window behind her mother's head.

"I could have him fired, you know," said Ivy. "You're only a child. He's taking advantage of you."

"I'll be eighteen in four months," said Cami, suddenly enraged. "You think I'm afraid of you?"

They scowled at one another from opposite ends of the table. The wind howled through the yard, rattling the windows in their frames. The house, for all its grandeur, was old and poorly insulated. Drafts crept beneath every door. The curtains fluttered, as if stirred by the icy fingers of passing ghosts.

Ivy sighed. She sipped from her water glass. Her temper was like that: rare, and short-lived.

"I've tried to raise you well." She spoke thoughtfully, as if to herself. "I've tried to keep you grounded. But time and again you prove yourself to be a stupid, petty girl. Your dad said you'd end up spoiled. I didn't believe him. He'd never been right about anything else."

Cami's rage, too, was fading. She felt like someone had reached inside and scooped out her guts.

"I have to fly to Tokyo tomorrow for a business meeting," said Ivy briskly. "I'll ask Justine to stay over a few nights. Joel will escort you to and from school."

"I don't need a babysitter."

"I disagree. All your life you've lived without restrictions, and where has it gotten you? You're failing three classes. You look half starved to death. It's time you benefited from some limitations."

There was no reason why the house should feel any emptier with Ivy in Tokyo than it had when she'd been in the city. But Cami wandered around the place listless as a phantom, slamming doors just to hear the noise echoing through the halls.

"Do you ever feel homesick in your own home?" she asked Marvin at the end of their tutoring session.

"Do you ever feel like you're going to flunk out of high school?" said Marvin.

Cami barely heard him. Friday was only two days away, and she agonized over what to do about Lucia. Ivy had taken away her credit card and instructed Justine to call the police if Cami snuck out of the house. Cami was sure there were ways to get around such restraints, but having been the beneficiary of a tremendously lax mothering style until now, she lacked the cunning of her peers who'd been outsmarting their parents since middle school. She stared at her mother's roadblocks and could see no way around. Maybe she didn't want to. Ever since the conversation in the kitchen, an unfamiliar resignation had settled inside her chest. It stunned her, how much she'd been hurt by Ivy's words. *Stupid-pet-ty-stupid-petty-stupid-petty.* The syllables pattered through her mind like rain plinking into a gutter.

Defeated, she called Lucia to tell her their meetings were suspended until further notice. The model did not pick up. Cami imagined her suffused in a crowd of glittering bodies and thought the jealousy would kill her.

After dinner, she resumed her restless roving through the house, clicking her magnetic fingertips together. What had seemed like a good idea at the time now struck her as embarrassing. The magnets were so weak, they adhered to nothing heavier than a paper clip. She could sneak back to the warehouse, ask for an upgrade, something more extreme. But the prospect of letting that creep slice her again flooded her with nausea. As she circled the great dining room table, running a palm across the polished tops of the chairs, Cami was disgusted to realize that, like Ivy, she had never wanted the implants in her own body. She had only wanted to enjoy them in the bodies of other people.

It was sheer luck that she happened to be on the first floor, and Justine upstairs taking a bath, when the knocker rapped against the front door. Somehow, Cami knew who it was even before she'd disabled the security system and Lucia spilled into the foyer. The model straightened up, laughing. She rotated in a full circle, gazing up at the crystal chandelier.

"So this is the queen's castle." She yanked a leafy frond from the potted palm tree by the door and brought it to her nose. "Fake!" she declared triumphantly. "Why am I not surprised?"

"What are you doing here?" asked Cami. Her delight at seeing Lucia warred with the panic simmering in her stomach. Even in her wildest fantasies, she had not dared to place the model here at the mansion where she so clearly did not belong.

"Your voicemail said you couldn't leave the house. I figured I'd come to you."

"How'd you get past the gate?"

"Climbed it. Your security man already left."

"You have to go."

"But I wanted to see you." She put on a false pout, or maybe a real one, leaned down, and kissed Cami on the corner of her lips. Cami felt her resistance slipping away.

"If Justine sees you . . ."

"Are you trying to tell me," said Lucia slyly, "that in this fucking fortress there's not a single place you can hide me?"

They hurried up several flights of stairs. Lucia tripped and laughed. Cami shushed her. Sound carried far along the house's empty walls. She realized that Lucia was drunk. They reached Ivy's attic office where Cami entered the four-digit code. "Wait here," she told Lucia. She raced back down the stairs in time to meet Justine, her long white neck poking swan-like out of the collar of her bathrobe, suspicious because she had heard the automated chimes of the security system as it turned off.

"It was Joel," invented Cami. "He wanted to know if we needed anything before he left."

"Did you tell him that window is sticking again?"

"I forgot."

Justine rolled her eyes and declared, for the third time, what an impressively light sleeper she was, how Cami should not even *dream* of trying to sneak out of the house during the night. As she wandered off to one of the guest rooms, it occurred to Cami, at last, that Justine had probably never liked her.

Lucia had found Ivy's spare glasses in the desk drawer. She wore them on the end of her nose as she lumbered around the office like a zombie. "I'm Ivy Morimoto. I'm the best cybernetic designer on the planet. I'm fucking infallible. Nobody can touch me." She raised her fingers to her mouth and mimed gnawing on the nails. Cami shut the door behind her. She was not amused. When you got down to it, she didn't believe anyone had a right to mock her mother other than herself.

"Where were you when I called?"

"Celebrating," said Lucia, collapsing into Ivy's swivel chair.

"Celebrating what?"

"I got fired. She must've found out we were fucking. I guess it wasn't hard to get a name once she knew the hotel." The glasses crunched in her hands as she crushed them.

"I thought you didn't care about losing your job. You said my mom was a has-been."

"Who said I cared?" Lucia found a pair of scissors and, using the plastic handles, began to hammer the lenses of Ivy's glasses into powder. "Ivy was a shitty employer. The way she looked down at all of us, like we were her personal robot slaves . . ." She lowered her face to the surface of the desk and blew, sending a sparkly rain of glass powder onto the carpet. "Rumor has it she's overseas looking for a buyer. Wants to cut her losses and sell. I'm one of the lucky ones. I'll be fine. I mean, look at me. I'm gorgeous." She stood. The sun had set, but the electric shine of the city crept through the windows, bathing her in a persistent, unhappy glow.

They made love on the plush white carpet, then fell asleep entwined, Lucia's open mouth expelling a cloying liquor stink. Cami's fingertips clung to the model's neck implant, but the attraction was so light, she couldn't tell whether it was the magnets or her imagination.

Sometime later, Cami awoke. She didn't know how long she'd been sleeping. The attic was chilly. She shivered as she sat up. She had spent the night in Ivy's office only once before. She was about six, and had fallen asleep at Ivy's feet while she worked at her desk. Then, too, Cami had awoken to find herself alone. Ivy had gone downstairs to bed and left her there, curled in a tight ball. Cami never knew whether her mother had just wanted to let her sleep, or whether Ivy had stepped over her still form without seeing her.

A shadow moved to Cami's left. She jumped to her feet and slapped the touch-activated lamp at her mother's desk. Light spilled over the scene: Cami with her hand still hovering by the lamp's base, and Lucia, rearing back from the brightness, a red leather notebook clutched in her left hand.

"Jesus, you scared me," said Cami. "What are you doing?"

"I couldn't sleep."

"I mean what are you doing with *that.*"

Lucia glanced down, as if she had only just noticed the notebook. The pages made a soft flapping sound as she flipped through them. Cami glimpsed her mother's cramped handwriting and human figures drawn in blue pen.

"I can't believe Ivy Morimoto sketches her designs by hand," said Lucia. "Doesn't she know it's the twenty-first century?"

"She's paranoid about getting hacked. She keeps everything hard copy until a design's ready to move forward." Cami shivered again. For the first time, she felt the gravity of what she had done, welcoming an outsider into her mother's space. She thought again of the surgeon in the warehouse. What would he pay to get his hands on Ivy's designs? Or to just plaster them all over the internet and embarrass her?

Lucia had turned the notebook sideways to examine a drawing of a torso sheathed in metal.

Cami held out her hand. "Give me the notebook."

Lucia grinned. "Seriously? I told you: Cyber fashion is dead. Nobody would want this trash anyway."

"Just give it to me."

She tried to take it. Lucia stepped away and raised the book out of reach. Her eyes shone with a cruel and mocking glint. Quickly, Cami accepted what she was willing to do in order to get the notebook back: the blows she would land, the fingernails scraping past hardware and digging into skin. They remained frozen that way for several moments until, with a dismissive flick of her metal wrist, the model sent the notebook spinning to the corner of the room. The carpet absorbed the impact. Lucia leaned against Ivy's desk, smug and beautiful as ever.

"Momma's girl through and through," she said.

It was a long, frosty walk down to the first floor where Cami deactivated the security system to let Lucia out of the house. Cami wondered without caring whether Justine would actually call the police. Discovering her empty bedroom, the front door carelessly left unlocked, Justine would think it no more than a daughter's brazen rebellion against a mother's control. But the truth was, watching Lucia vanish through the gates without looking back, Cami could summon no resentment for Ivy. She thought of her mother sleepwalking around her Japanese hotel room, ankles thudding against so much unfamiliar furniture.

A feeling of loss built in Cami, but slowly. She didn't feel the full force of it until an hour later when she'd arrived at the apartment Andrew shared with three other college guys, and he, groggy but gratified to see her, led her down the hall to his bed.

Afterward, they lay quietly beneath the blankets, listening to the gurgling of the pipes inside the walls. The heat rolling from Andrew onto Cami's naked side was like a steaming wet towel. Tears slid down her face. Andrew reached out to touch one where it dangled off the edge of her jaw.

"Did I hurt you?" he asked.

Cami shook her head. As if she could be hurt by such clumsy, primitive flesh.

THE LINE

FOR ALMOST AN HOUR they'd held their positions: he sitting on the floor watching the wardrobe, and she, sitting on the bed, watching him. His green eyes were scrunched nearly shut. Her palms rested on her knees. It was as if they were posing for a painting: Girl & Cat, or maybe Girl Studies Cat. The only flaw in the tableau was the tip of Cornelius's tail, fidgeting like an insect on the scuffed tile.

Outside, the occasional bang of a door or drawer cut through the student chatter. It all sounded suspiciously fuzzy to Alice, like a recording wheezing from an old tape deck. Her own room lacked the movie posters and stick-on whiteboards she'd glimpsed her classmates slapping to cinder blocks on the four trips it'd taken her to unload the car. Her conditions for going to college had been twofold: 1) A doctor's note wrung from a sympathetic shrink, classifying Cornelius a therapy pet and green-lighting his living in the dorm; and 2) her parents could not accompany her on move-in. The latter stung, she knew; her older brother had never made it to college, so for Don and Mae, Alice's matriculation oozed the syrupy sentiment of the first baby bird flapping from the nest.

But the last two years had sapped her independence. Between the surgeries and the recovery and the rehab, she'd hardly had a second to herself. She craved an experience all her own, a new place unsullied by the well-intentioned dirt of family. Eventually, she'd gotten Mae on her side, and outnumbered, Don had folded. Alice packed her dinged-up gold Civic with three milk crates, a litter box, and a duffel bag, and backed out of her parents' driveway while they stood waving on the porch, their jaws fixed into fake smiles.

Cornelius's ears twitched as a fist began hammering the door.

"Hey! This is Nicole, your orientation leader!" Alice imagined a thin, overzealous girl with a bright green lanyard and a ponytail. "We're all headed to the dining hall for a floor dinner. Wanna come along? It's taco night!"

Alice didn't move. She sucked in air and held it. *One, two, three* . . . By the time she'd gotten to thirty-seven, the floor had dropped into blessed silence.

She got up slowly, creaking like an old lady. The sunlight pouring through the window had pinned Cornelius in a rectangle of gold. Nudging him aside, she gripped the wardrobe's handles and yanked. A gust of musty-smelling air whooshed out to meet her. Nothing inside, except a smeary mirror bolted to the left-hand door, and down below, a solitary maple leaf.

Alice twirled it by the stem. Though it was late August and the trees beyond her window still glowed a vibrant green, this leaf was a mottled orange-red, darkening to crimson at its points. She dug inside a milk crate until she found a roll of packing tape. She peeled off a strip and stuck the leaf to the door. Her very first decoration.

"Wellness check."

Alice froze, one hand wrapped around the cup of instant noodles she was about to place in the microwave. It was the indeterminate hour between breakfast and lunch. She'd slept late, fed Cornelius, then lazed around in bed alternating between her *Big Book of Sudoku* and her Instagram feed, all without granting one thought toward the world beyond the third floor of this red-brick residence hall. And now here was the world, knocking.

She waited. Cornelius dozed on the windowsill, his paws fluttering as he raced his way through a dream. If he resented his confinement after years of free reign of Alice's parents' house, he didn't show it. He was content to stay in this room forever, not wanting or needing a thing from anyone outside. The man in the hall exhaled.

"Listen, if you're alive in there, please open up. Else I gotta come busting in, and no girl wants that."

Alice set down the noodles and went to the door. The man on the other side was tall, bearded, and Black, with a gaudy silver crucifix hanging from a chain around his neck. A yellow patch on the arm of his sky-blue T-shirt read CAMPUS SAFETY.

"So," he said, with satisfaction. "You are alive."

"Why wouldn't I be?"

"I got a report here that says you were a no-show to new student orientation."

"All that summer camp stuff isn't really for me."

"You also missed your first day of class."

Shoot. What day was it, even? She'd completely lost track of time.

"I don't even have my textbooks," admitted Alice.

"The bookstore can help with that. Grab your keycard. I'll show you."

It was much cooler outside than in her dorm room. The sunshine was so bright. Alice wrapped her arms around the cardigan she'd thrown over her camisole, feeling like someone's invalid aunt hauled outside for a day trip. The campus safety officer was big as a linebacker but walked with a monk's serenity, hands clasped behind his back. A few kids waved and cried out versions of, "How's it hangin', Gus?" He smiled and shouted generic greetings in reply. Alice didn't know what to make of all the goodwill. At her high school, the security guards had been big, mean assholes with crew cuts, standing beside the metal detector each morning like gargoyles flanking a castle gate.

They reached a building with a handful of café tables scattered under a green awning.

"Ta-da!" said Gus, spreading his arms. "You just go in there and show them your course list. They'll get you sorted."

"Thanks," said Alice. "And uhh—the dining hall?"

He looked at her with an unreadable expression. She felt her stupidity sucking her into its mouth like quicksand. He went into the building and returned with a black-and-white campus map. He spread it against the bookstore window and penned circles around a few locations: library, dining hall, fitness center.

"It can take some time to settle in," said Gus quietly as Alice studied the map. "But just be patient. There are good people here."

She found the textbooks for her four classes. She turned away from a large display of highlighters and note cards, knowing there were cheaper supplies at the Walmart in town—before remembering she had money now. The settlement had been finalized in the spring and it was still so new to her, this concept that she need not scrutinize every price tag. She bought a pack of highlighters, two composition notebooks, a box of fancy organic fruit snacks, and an overpriced baseball tee with the college logo splashed across the front.

By the time she got back to the residence hall, she felt happy and normal: just a regular college student returning from some errands. She tossed her bags on the bed, where Cornelius had relocated. He was watching the wardrobe again. He'd been doing that a lot over the past few days. Alice wondered if he was getting a little senile in his old age.

According to her course schedule, she had an hour before her next class. She would use the time to unpack. She found a bunch of metal hangers her mom had Scotch-taped together and wedged into one of the milk crates. She stepped forward and opened the wardrobe doors. Out puffed a second leaf, as if borne on a breeze or a person's long exhalation. Cornelius pounced, batting it around the room. It was so like the first leaf, Alice turned to check that it was still stuck to her door.

She ran her hands across every bit of the wardrobe, standing on a milk crate to reach the top shelf. Only when she'd reassured herself that it was completely empty did she begin hanging up her clothes.

She had to admit it was better, being involved. Alone in her dorm room, she'd been like a hapless water creature dithering on the sand, too disoriented to realize she was drying out. Now the currents were sweeping her smoothly along. She went to her classes. She ate her meals in the dining hall. She walked through the student activity fair where classmates waved their flags and free candy. Alice put her name on the email list for the board game club, not because she cared for games especially, but because she liked the way the club president smiled at her as she pressed a Tootsie Roll into Alice's hand.

She even surprised herself by attending her first party, if you could call it that. A door down the hall from hers hung open. A gangly boy wearing neon swim trunks, sunglasses, and nothing else stood outside holding a beer can, toasting everyone that passed: "Come on in, come on in, the water's fine!" Inside, Alice discovered a fire-code-defying assemblage of fifteen or eighteen people. Someone passed her a warm beer. She located a free patch of floor against the dresser and struck up a conversation with a tall blonde she recognized from Pre-Calc. It was unbearably warm in the overcrowded room. The air reeked of alcohol, sweat, and funky boy odor. Alice drained the beer and a second one appeared like magic.

"What happened to your head?" asked the blonde, whose name was Savannah. She sounded merely curious. Alice touched the rubbery pink worm on the side of her skull where no hair would grow.

"I got in a car accident."

"Must've been a bad one."

"It was." Alice sipped from the beer, remembering. "I was in the hospital a long time. I needed seven surgeries. Rehab took a whole year. And my brother, Cleo—he was killed."

As soon as she said it she realized her mistake. Panic glazed Savannah's already glassy eyes, and the boy in the swim trunks, who'd been eavesdropping, declared, "Oh shit!" Heads swiveled toward them. Alice felt a flush creeping up her neck. Muttering something about the bathroom, she stumbled through the forest of outstretched legs and dove into the hall.

She found herself outside without understanding how she'd gotten there. In the days after the accident, time had often played tricks on her, morphine sanding off the boundaries between scenes, dumping her into conversations without beginning or end. Rain pattered the sidewalk. People slid past in the darkness like ghost ships. Those two cheep beers had hit harder than she'd anticipated. She never would've started blabbering about Cleo had she been in her right mind.

Now it was as if his name had unlocked a strongbox buried deep inside her guts. Out surged the goose honk of his laughter, the cigarette smell of his hair, the lurid green nail polish he'd wear to school just to upset their father. He was seven years older than Alice, a bright moon orbiting the dull rock of home. Sometimes she felt at peace with his death, and sometimes, the remembered brilliance of him had her starry-eyed and stupid, stunned into immobility like an animal stranded in the middle of the road.

Alice called her parents. Her mother snatched up the phone midway through the first ring.

"How are you? Is everything okay? How are your classes? The food? Did you make friends? Is everything okay?"

"Everything is fine." Alice leaned back on her bed with her cell phone resting on her stomach and the cat nestled between her knees. It was Saturday morning, the building steeped in an achy hungover quiet. She'd been out most of the night, just walking through the rain and thinking about her brother. "Do you remember what sort of tree it was that we hit?"

"What?"

"The tree. Me and Cleo."

During the first few months Mae had wept any time her son's name was mentioned. Now she just sounded annoyed. "I have no idea."

"Is Dad home? Can you ask him?"

"Is this really—?"

"Please. Just ask him." If anyone knew, it would be Don. He had a mind for details like that, the sort of man who could tell you what shirt he was wearing last Tuesday, or identify a backyard bird based on the slightest flare of color between branches.

A faint clunk sounded as Mae set down the receiver. Alice waited, tracing two fingers down the soft fur behind Cornelius's whiskers, until her mother returned.

"Your father says he has no idea."

"Could it have been a maple?" She faced her closed door, and the leaves stuck side by side like two weird eyeballs. Her memory of the collision was spotty, but she knew Cleo's car had rolled down a hillside and smashed into a huge old tree. She knew that she had dangled upside-down for what seemed like days, harnessed by her seat belt, trying to decipher the secret code of the wet leaves plastered to the windshield.

Mae took in a large, steadying breath. "If it's too soon, Alice. If it feels like too much . . . You could take classes at the community college, work toward an associate degree."

"I'm fine." Cornelius cracked open an eye, irked by the harshness in her voice. "I have to go now, Mom. My friends are meeting me for brunch."

She ended the call. Outside her window, blue jays screamed. A dumpster lid slammed. Alice swung her legs out of bed and regarded the floor, streaky with the mud she'd tracked in a few hours ago when she finally found her way back to the residence hall. But something was wrong: Her feet were size six—doll's feet, Mae used to say in exasperation as Alice's heels popped out of the backs of all the tried-on sneakers in the shoe store. The muddy prints on her dorm room floor were large. Like a man's. Like a boy trying to be a man. Like a boy who was shamefully extravagant about his footwear, who'd blow his paycheck on pills and a pair of Nike Joyrides and then show up stoned on his parents' front porch at 2:00 a.m. and bang on the door slurring "Memory" from *Cats* until one of their parents let him in—until the night they didn't. Until the night Alice staggered out of bed to find her parents bickering in the hall, Cleo pounding at the door, and what was it her mother had been hissing to her father over and over? *You asked me where the line was and it's right here. We're standing on it. This is it.*

She spent less and less time in her dorm room. Cornelius grew resentful, depositing revenge hairballs in the hard-to-reach corners under the bed. If it hadn't been for the cat, she might never have come back. She would've crashed in the library's twenty-four-hour room with the procrastinators pulling all-nighters, or pitched a tent in the woods behind the football field.

But who was to say it would've made any difference? Cleo had never been one for boundaries or rules. For all Alice knew, she would've woken in her tent to the same screeching tire sound from her dreams. Maple leaves would've trailed her into the library, slithering into her open backpack the moment she turned away.

One night in early October while emptying the litter box, Alice straightened and dropped the scooper with a clatter, certain she'd heard her brother's wail as the car tipped over the lip of the hill and started rolling. Half a second later, the sound clarified into someone's joyful shriek down in the parking lot, followed by a hiss and a pop. Fireworks. Alice went to the window and watched the spitting glow of sparklers in the darkness until her heart rate slowed.

On her way to the dumpster, she ran into Gus. The security officer leaned contentedly against a street lamp like he hung out there all the time.

"Hello Alice. You taking care? What've you got there?"

"Cat shit." She shifted the plastic bag to her other hand. "Busy night for you."

"They're all busy."

"No one ever gets in any trouble." She had observed this over the past few weekends. Security swept through the building, waving their flashlights and ejecting kids from overloaded rooms. On occasion they might make an underage student dump his beer down the sink drain. That was it.

Gus shrugged. "We're not the cops. We're not trying to ruin anyone's good time. Nobody makes it to adulthood without being forgiven for dumb mistakes."

That had been true enough for Cleo, according to her mother: forgiven and forgiven again. Even after a brief stint in juvie his records were sealed. Blank slate. A thousand and one chances to make amends.

A breeze cut across the parking lot, wet and reeking of sulfur. Alice glimpsed the crucifix around Gus's neck.

"Do you believe in the afterlife?"

"I do."

She liked how calmly he answered, as if she'd asked whether he enjoyed coffee or had a Hulu subscription. The way she'd grown up, religion, like politics, was a fraught and nasty subject, best avoided unless you wanted to piss everybody off.

"My dad was a minister," explained Gus.

"So you never really had any choice."

"Oh, there's always a choice."

"Do you believe in ghosts?"

Gus tipped his head back against the lamp post, the light beaming down into his upturned face. "Ghosts, no," he said after a pause. "Angels and devils, yes."

"I don't believe in any of that," said Alice. "Or—well—I didn't."

"That's the funny thing about faith." He looked at her, blinking hard, and Alice knew he was struggling to see beyond the light's bright afterimage unfurling in his vision. "You don't believe until something happens, and then you do."

Alice walked up the stairs slowly, thinking it over. Was Cleo an angel or a devil? She'd been asking herself versions of that question for as long as she could remember. It seemed to Alice that Cleo had two very different people living inside him. There was the rude, impulsive, selfish mess of a boy—her parents' son—who had to be evicted from the household for his little sister's own good, a terrible role model, drug addict, chummy with all sorts of small-time criminals. And then there was the spry young person brimming with love and laughter—Alice's brother—who'd smuggle her out of middle school midday for Wendy's and an R-rated movie, who'd listen to her adolescent grievances with the patience of a priest, then swear vengeance on her enemies with the zeal of a Renaissance lover.

One time, her sixth grade geometry teacher, Mr. Rackowski, had refused to let Alice visit the bathroom during class. The resultant blood stain on the crotch of her gym shorts was a gleeful talking point for days. Alice didn't remember telling Cleo about the incident, but she must have, for shortly thereafter, someone slashed every tire of Rackowski's Subaru in the school parking lot and carved DICK in large letters onto the hood of the car.

And how had she repaid him for his loyalty? By shutting him out. By believing her parents' lies. That night Mae and Don had refused to let him inside, Alice could've pushed past them and opened the door. At the very least she could've snuck around the back of the house and met him out front, talked to him, made sure he knew she was still on his side. But she was eighteen, she was thinking about the future. The more she mulled over those college application questions about personal growth and formative experiences, the more a belated resentment slunk through her like illness. She realized how fully the shadow of Cleo had eclipsed her childhood, her parents' attention fixed always on fixing him, on preventing Alice from becoming like him. She didn't know a thing about herself that was not in opposition to her brother: good daughter, nice girl, the one who'd make her parents proud.

Back in her room, Alice emptied out the wardrobe, yanking clothes off their hangers. Another maple leaf fluttered out, this one shriveled and crunchy. Cornelius joined her on the floor. They sat, watching the open doors together, long after the second round of sparklers had been deployed and the campus extinguished into silence.

Alice began stocking her room with her brother's favorite things. She didn't have the patience to sit and make a list, which was just as well. There was something fitting about shopping for these items Cleo-style, dashing into town between classes or at weird hours of the night to snatch a jumbo bag of jalapeño cheese puffs, a shiny new pair of sneakers, or a tube of that smelly acne ointment he used to keep in his car and shove into Alice's hands each time a zit bloomed on her forehead.

She was on her way back from one of these haphazard shopping trips when she got to her door and couldn't find her keycard. She stood in the hallway, uselessly patting herself down while Cornelius cried on the other side. Someone poked her head out of the communal bathroom.

"Is that a baby?"

"He thinks so." Alice sifted through her shopping bags one at a time in case the card had fallen inside. She looked over her shoulder again. It was Savannah. Of all the people to be stuck in the hallway with, it had to be the person she'd embarrassed herself in front of. They hadn't spoken since that first party weeks ago.

"What are you looking for?"

"My keycard. I must've dropped it on the way in."

"I do that all the time." Savannah stepped out of the bathroom and let the door swing shut behind her. "You've just got to retrace your steps. I'll help!"

They descended the musty, echoing stairwells and followed the track of orange carpet around the first floor to the north exit. Savannah kept her eyes on the ground and Alice kept her eyes on Savannah, wondering why she was being so nice. In the parking lot, Alice unlocked her car and they crawled around for a minute until Savannah emitted a triumphant shout: There it was, lying under the backseat where it must have fallen while she loaded her groceries, Alice's bleary-eyed portrait scowling through a window of clear plastic.

Savannah helped her carry the remaining bags upstairs. In Alice's room she cooed over Cornelius, who gave her a disinterested onceover before stalking under the bed.

"Thanks for your help," said Alice.

"No worries." Savannah's eyes slid from the gaping wardrobe to the pile of clothing in the corner of the room, but she didn't ask. "Do you have a fake?" she added, as Alice slid a six-pack of Cleo's favorite Pilsner into the mini-fridge.

"I turned twenty-one over the summer."

"What!"

"I had to take a few years off after high school."

The implications of this statement hung in the air like smog. Savannah picked up a feathered cat toy and tossed it from hand to hand.

"I want to apologize."

"For what?"

"I was like, really insensitive when you told me about your brother. You know how your brain just shuts off when you aren't sure what to say?" She threw the toy onto the floor. Cornelius's paw drifted out from beneath the bed and gave it an experimental swat. "I think I know a little bit of what you're going through. My stepdad died of cancer when I was twelve."

"Really?"

She nodded. It should have been a heavy admission, yet Alice felt a succession of tight knots within herself sliding loose.

"How did you get over it?"

"I don't think I did. I don't think I ever could. I mean, my favorite person was gone. Do you ever really get over a thing like that?"

Alice didn't have an answer. She opened the fridge and grabbed two Pilsners, one for herself and one for Savannah. She thought Cleo wouldn't mind.

Halloween had always been Alice's favorite holiday. Christmas and Thanksgiving were sad and insular affairs, especially without Cleo, the house pressing in on her and her parents like the rounded walls of a snow globe. But on Halloween the world felt a little bigger. It was like a hidden window had opened in a stuffy bedroom, bringing in moonlight and forest smells, the promise of the unknown.

According to myparanormalodyssey.net, which Alice had bookmarked on her laptop, Halloween was also the day when the line between the living and the dead was thinnest. Things slipped from one side to the other with ease. Some cultures acknowledged this by spending the day cleaning gravestones and praying for relatives stuck in purgatory. Not so in this dumb country. Even now, with hours to go till sundown, kids hurtled around the hall in half-assed costumes and makeup already starting to smear.

At Savannah's request, Alice had bought alcohol for the floor: four bottles of wine, a fat green jug of gin, two liters of tonic. She didn't expect to be paid back, but around six, she opened her door to a person draped in a bed sheet, their palm unfolding around a sheaf of damp dollar bills. More classmates came by. A girl in a leotard and cat ears. The gangly boy from the first party who'd added flippers and goggles to his swim trunks.

"You'll be cold," said Alice, feeling like a buzzkill mom.

"Baby, I'm on fire," slurred the boy, who had already sampled the gin. He tottered away, flippers slapping. Alice added the money to her Cleo-shrine, a collection of items piled in front of the open wardrobe like a clumsy offering to a hungry god.

Darkness fell. The building tipped into a chaos that made past weekends seem docile as church retreats. People screamed in fun or terror. Stereos pounded clashing rhythms that shook the walls. From the parking lot came the repeated sound of glass breaking, as if someone had a boxful of vases and was just hurling them against the ground. Savannah came by once, shouting through the door, begging her to come join the fun. Alice lit three votive candles and stuck them in the wardrobe. The shadows squirmed over the walls like wiggling fingers. She didn't know what she was doing. She wasn't a minister or a medium. She was a dead man's little sister, and she wanted the impossible to come true.

Sirens finally stirred her from her vigil. She'd heard them approaching for the last few minutes, but once they were under her window, they were impossible to ignore. She got to her feet, legs aching, and leaned into the hall where the overhead lights dazzled her eyes. When had it gotten so quiet? A big white donut of industrial toilet paper lay on its side just outside the bathroom. Someone's mask had been stripped off and abandoned: a grotesque reptilian face with a crown of flaccid spikes.

Alice heard people murmuring. She rounded the corner and the crowd of waiting monsters melted to admit her passage. The door to the floor's second bathroom was propped open. Two flippered feet protruded from the handicap shower stall. A girl was in there with him, doing CPR.

"She went to lifeguard camp," explained a boy in a unicorn onesie, the self-appointed narrator of this tragedy.

Alice couldn't stand the way they were all loitering there like rubbernecks gawking at a highway pileup. She went back to her side of the hall and slumped against the wall, feeling worse and worse, until the noise of the EMTs clattering up the stairwell spooked her into her room.

Fire. Her room was on fire. The flames stretched from the base of the wardrobe to the pile of Cleo's offerings a foot and a half away. For a minute, Alice could do nothing but watch, mesmerized, as the bag of cheese puffs curled and smoldered. Then a door banged somewhere and she was jolted back into her body. She seized a towel from her hamper and leapt, stamping hard with her shower flip-flops until the last bit of orange had been snuffed out.

She sank into the ruins, a rank, burnt plastic smell tingling in her nostrils. The wardrobe doors were shut tight. She didn't understand what had happened. Had Cleo rejected her gifts? Did the cat pounce on a candle in those few minutes she'd been out of the room?

"Cornelius?"

She heard him stirring under the bed, but he wouldn't come out.

Too tired to make sense of any of it, Alice slipped under the covers fully dressed and closed her eyes. Still she could see the Martian glow of the ambulance lights pressing against the window. Flippers was young. He would be fine. They'd pump his stomach at the hospital like they did for Cleo that one time, and he'd wake feeling like shit, embarrassed, lucky to be alive.

Unless he didn't, and Alice went to jail.

"Cleo," she said aloud. "I really messed up."

I'm coming to get you. That's what he would've said if she'd had him on the phone. Because no matter how fucked up his life, no matter how much money he'd blown through or people he'd steamrolled on his ever-deepening plunge toward the next mistake, Cleo would've moved worlds to help her.

Predictably, her aloofness had lasted only as long as it took her to need him again. Eight weeks she ignored his texts and snubbed his covert visits, and then her girlfriend dumped her for a basketball player and suddenly Alice wanted only for Cleo to take her out, sneak her into a bar, distract her from the tiny problems of her mundane life. He came to her rescue. As if she hadn't spent the past two months being a total jerk, he swooped into the driveway and laid on the horn, launching the neighbor's hound dogs into a fit of howling. Alice entered the car through the back and climbed over the divider into the front seat because the passenger door handle was held together with duct tape, and off they sped in that clattering junk heap, Cleo without a seatbelt because he never wore a seatbelt, the two of them laughing, laughing, right up to the moment the stranger's Lexus drifted over the yellow lines and bowled them over the side of the hill, and the irony of it all was that Cleo was ten days sober. He got like that sometimes: little bursts of purity, juice fast, cigarettes in the trash.

"This is it," he'd told her. "I'm getting it right this time. Are you ready to meet Cleo 2.0?"

"I'm ready," said Alice, opening her eyes. She must have drifted off. Music and shouting filled the hallway once more. How could they keep partying like nothing had happened? And then Alice thought: How could they not? No one wanted to make room for loss, the way it went rudely on and on.

The ambulance had departed, but as Alice sat up a light flared in her room, two lights, twin beams blazing with blinding intensity. She lifted her hands to shield her eyes, and between her woven fingers, caught a glimpse of Cornelius perched on the edge of the dresser, staring calmly at the wardrobe from which the brightness emanated. Over the sound of her classmates' merry-making, Alice heard the purr of an idling engine.

"I'm ready," she said again. She got to her feet and reached for the doors.

THE RUNAWAY RESTAURANT

BEFORE MY DAUGHTER RAN away, she stood in the kitchen with a hand on the patio door. I had just Windexed. Max knew this. I saw the cruel satisfaction lighting her eyes as she smeared fingerprints across the glass.

"I mean it," she said. "I'm leaving. And you're going to regret it. You're gonna remember this moment for the rest of your life."

She wore gray sweatpants, Converse sneakers, and a red Linkin Park T-shirt I would later recall in detail for the police. Sweat had sculpted her short hair into spikes. Twenty minutes ago, we'd been sealed peacefully in our separate spheres: Max in the basement, taped fists thundering a punching bag; and I in the kitchen, chopping tomatoes for a dinner she now refused to eat.

"Go ahead," I snapped. "Let's see how long you last out there. Please. You'd be doing me a favor."

Her lips compressed, rolled inward, as if in her fury she were trying to devour her own mouth. This was something she got from me. It meant a lot, when your kid was adopted, to see the gestures they picked up. From Rhonda, Maxine learned to pick her fingernails, to overuse air quotes, to toss her head back dramatically each time she swallowed a pill. In her anger, though, Max was all mine. Maybe that's why we fought so much. Rage as common ground. We fought over curfews and car privileges—the usual sites of mother-daughter contention—and then we fought over things that didn't matter, over Advil versus Aleve and the merits of yoga and whether a sweater was blue-green or just regular green. Rhonda, a sweet, pacifying person who lay awake worrying about her failing trig students, didn't understand how these fights could fill me with simultaneous fury and joy. My blood sang in my ears as I screamed. Often I collapsed into hiccupping laughter the moment Max left the room.

The night that she ran—a March night, still stiff with winter's chill—and disappeared across the patio, we'd been fighting over food. Max said she wanted to go vegan. I said she could eat whatever the hell I cooked and be grateful for it. The fight was briefer than usual. Max fled before I'd reached the bone-quaking peak of my volume. As I slid the tomatoes into the skillet, I suffered a sense of letdown. I had thought there would be more.

At first it brought Rhonda and me together, the way unexpected loss sometimes does. We returned to the streets of Tacoma long after the local search parties had disbanded for the night, our bathrobes flapping beneath the hems of our winter coats. We visited our parents—mine in Kansas City, hers out in Rhode Island. We ate our mothers' food and endured our fathers' blank-eyed smiles. We weren't having sex anymore, but we held hands all the time.

She said, "I don't blame you. It's not your fault."

And then she sobbed and said, "This is all your fault!"

And then she didn't say anything. For weeks on end, she had nothing to say. That was when I knew it was over.

She accepted a teaching position at some SUNY I'd never heard of. I stayed behind, quit my admin job at Puget Sound, and became one of those unaffiliated drifters that hangs about college towns. I had some savings, enough for a year, more if I stopped eating. My former colleague, Nathan, stopped by once a week with his wife, Gwen. "To get you out of the house," he said. They bustled me around on day trips—museums, parks, the movies, the library—as if I were an ailing relative whose care had fallen into their hands.

I did like going to the public library. I hadn't been since Max was little and we switched over to the university one for convenience's sake. You would've thought I'd been depressed, holding the same sticky copy of *The Snowy Day* my daughter once clasped in her fingers. But in the library, I discovered a quietude of self-hatred that was almost like peace. I took pleasure in the dusty silence, punctuated now and then by a cough or a child's squeal, and the smell of stillness that hung between the stacks.

Struck by my frequent visits (and probably guilt-tripped by Nathan), the head librarian, Frank, offered me a job. I nearly turned it down. I was wary of making attachments to new people and places that might vanish just as Max had vanished into the night. In the end, through a combination of pleading and absurd flattery regarding my bookkeeping skills, Nathan convinced me to give it a try. I'm grateful he did. Without that job, I never would have met Lacey, the girl who told me about the runaway restaurant.

She didn't call it that. She didn't remember its name. Runaway restaurant was something I came up with on my own. It was the place where all the kids who'd run away from home ended up, sooner or later. For some it was a pit stop. Get yourself a hot shower, a grilled cheese sandwich, and then you were on your way. Others lingered. Took on odd jobs while they figured out where to head next. Lacey had been one of them.

"I was the youngest kid there, seven or eight," she recalled as we shelved biographies one afternoon. She didn't say what she'd run away from, and I didn't ask. "There wasn't a whole lot I could do, but I tried. I would sweep, refill drinks, pick the gum off the bottoms of the chairs."

Lacey was a twenty-something of indeterminate origins with twelve facial piercings and a slash of dyed yellow hair. Yesterday, she overheard Frank talking with someone about Maxine's disappearance, which had just reached its two-year anniversary. That was when she remembered the runaway restaurant.

"What—you just forgot about it?" I asked.

"It's sorta like that," said Lacey. "I think they design it that way on purpose. So people don't go around blabbing about it once they've come and gone."

She took a Churchill biography, consulted the call number, and wiggled it into place. I stared unseeingly at the spine of the book in my hand. Lacey struck me as someone who'd done a lot of drugs. Her brain was probably fried. She didn't know what she was talking about. Or else this runaway restaurant was a fantasy she'd invented to help cope with some trauma, the way lonely children cling to imaginary friends.

We finished shelving the books and rolled the cart back to the elevator. The shadows of snowflakes drifted across the carpeted aisles.

"This restaurant," I said as Lacey jabbed the down button. "Is it nearby?"

"Nah. Somewhere east, near where I grew up in New York. And north, I think." She gestured vaguely toward the library's paneled wood ceiling. "Yeah. There was a Canadian or two in the mix. They used to stop in for a bite after they made it across the border."

"But you don't know where exactly? You don't have the name of the town?"

"I told you, it doesn't work like that. They design—"

"They design it that way on purpose. I remember."

The elevator dinged. The doors juddered open and Lacey rolled the cart inside. My chest felt heavy, stuffed with wet wool. There was this grief counselor Rhonda and I had seen a few times, a Latina woman with a kind, doughy face and ink stains on her slacks. She used to talk about grief as if it were a drug addiction. You could suffer relapses. Without warning, you'd be wallowing in old agonies for days.

Lacey sighed and clattered her ringed fingers against the cart's handles. "It's only the runaways who can find it. The runaway kids." She said it under her breath, like a prayer. She looked at me with glazed blue eyes. "If you can find one, maybe they can lead you to it."

Nathan and Gwen were pleasantly surprised at the prospect of my road trip. Four weeks, I told them, to visit family in Missouri. They agreed to look after the house—no real burden, once I stopped the mail and let all the plants die. I arranged to take the time off work, which is to say, I announced my intentions to Frank eighteen hours before I departed, and he shrugged a shoulder and said *bon voyage*, because there's no use arguing with a crazy person.

I drove through the streets of Tacoma just before dawn on a Tuesday, a half-empty duffel tossed in the back seat. A slushy rain had fallen during the night. Streetlamps cast murky orange circles on the wet roads. Along the bay, massive cranes hung over the silhouettes of scrap metal ships. I got out of the car and stood beside the brightening water, replaying for the millionth time the scene of Max's leaving, certain, as always, that if I got the details just right, I could prevent it from ever having happened.

Where could she have gone? It was a question Rhonda and I had turned over and over back when we were still together. The fears, too dreadful to name, and the delusions: Max lounging on a boat with a Coke sweating on her stomach; Max skiing down a steep slope, goggled and grinning. She had never expressed any desire to travel. Her school friends said they had no idea where she might have gone, though they admitted Max had "changed" in the past six months, grown crabby and secretive, slouched into soccer practice late so many times the coach had threatened to suspend her. Teachers, too, recounted my daughter's quieting—though her grades remained steady, she had relocated to desks in the back of the room, separating herself from classmates.

"Why didn't we know about any of this?" I exploded at

Rhonda one night. "Why didn't anyone tell us?" I paced back and forth before the open window. She sat on the bed, squeezing hydrocortisone from a flattened tube. Stress hives bloomed on her belly and arms. She swigged liquid Benadryl at every meal, stumbled around with a glassy, irritated look in her eyes.

"There are a thousand students in that school," she snapped. "They can't possibly track the behavior of every one. Max is our responsibility. Not theirs." I sank onto the bed, forehead pressed to my palms. She softened, then rubbed my back and said, "I didn't notice anything different about her, either."

The sun was rising. I got back in the car and flipped down the visor against the glare. I wasn't going to Missouri. I entered Rhonda's new address in New York, though I didn't plan on going there, either. I just needed a destination point that would get me east. East and north. For the time being, this was enough.

But I had underestimated my own reluctance to sit in a car for twelve hours. That first day, I made it only as far as Missoula before crapping out in a Comfort Inn, kneading the knots in my shoulders beneath a lukewarm shower spray. The second day, severe thunderstorms blackened the sky. A wall of rain raced in from the west, and my slashing wipers couldn't clear it. I fell two hundred miles short of my goal of Bismarck and spent another restless night on an overpriced mattress, blinking away the afterimage of highway unspooling beneath my eyelids.

I tried not to think about Lacey or her restaurant. When I inevitably did, I felt so mortified I nearly leapt into my car and sped back to Washington. I must have been losing my mind. What else could explain why I was driving 3,000 miles to track down a magical restaurant on the word of a coworker who struggled to alphabetize DVDs? Yes: I'd gone off the deep end. Blown a gasket. Cracked. And in this realization, there was relief. The daily drives became easier. I slept better at night. I really believed I could do this. I could bring our daughter home. It was sometime during this period that I invented the name runaway restaurant and started to dream about Max secure within its walls. At night, I watched cooking shows on hotel TVs, collecting images of comfort: flaky breads and gleaming tomatoes; piles of lemon zest; soup, thick with potatoes, bubbling in big iron pots.

At a rest stop near Cleveland, I took it upon myself to call Rhonda. I could count on one hand the number of times we'd talked since separating. But there at the picnic table behind the building with the McDonald's and the restrooms and the arcade, a clean, sharp breeze blowing in off Lake Erie and seagulls picking through the trash, I was pleased to hear her voice.

"I'm at work," she said. "Are you all right?"

"I'm great." Snow lay around the table, stamped with the footprints of people who'd come and gone. Someone had drawn a smiley face with the tip of a finger. I stooped to add buckteeth and horns, the way Max would've done if she were here. "I've got this job at the library—well, I'm not there now. I'm actually taking a bit of a drive. I'm in Ohio. Did you ever notice how many flags they've got along the highways? Like you need to be constantly reminded you're in the US. Do they do that in other countries, or is that just an American ego thing?"

A pause. I heard what was either the rustling of papers, or the static of a bad connection. "Did you say Ohio? Where are you going?"

"Don't know. Wherever the wind takes me."

More rustling. Definitely static. Rhonda's voice came out tinny and small, as if she were speaking through a metal pipe. "You don't sound right, Dee. If you're driving east, why don't you come stay with me for a night or two . . . Are you alone?"

"Are you?" I asked. I told myself it didn't matter. What was it to me if Rhonda had found some other woman to swirl hydrocortisone over the elusive patch in the center of her back? But my optimism was curdling. I wished I hadn't called. "I have to go now," I said before she could respond. "I'll call you."

I hung up and stood there looking at the water. The hand that had been clutching the phone burned with cold. As I made my way back to the parking lot, I resolved not to call Rhonda again, and not to pick up if she called me. I wouldn't speak to her until I had news about Max.

When I entered New York, my GPS began to admonish me for my refusal to leave I-90 and take the route to Rhonda's place. I unplugged it and threw it into the backseat. I felt sore, unwashed, and bloated from the fast food that had sustained me since leaving Tacoma. But I wasn't without hope. In five days, I had traversed nearly the length of the country, a feat of which I would not have believed myself capable a year ago. The worst was behind me. Now I only needed a hitchhiker.

I left the thruway, and for two days wandered the serpentine back roads of farm country still in the grips of winter. Jacketed figures shoveled snow from around mailboxes. Horses tugged carriages along the side of the road, capped and bonneted children peeking out the back. The two or three hitchhikers I did encounter were men with large backpacks and beards and hoods pulled up against the chill, and I needed a teenager, someone young whose plight would open up the avenue to the runaway restaurant.

On the eighth day since leaving Tacoma, I met a friendly trucker at a rest stop who informed me that hitchhiking had gone out of fashion, so to speak. Travelers were traumatized by tales of abduction and murder, while more and more companies forbade their drivers from offering rides to strangers. It was not what I wanted to hear. I sought to convince myself that it was just the cold weather preventing the surge of appropriately aged hitchhikers from appearing.

I checked into a hotel near Poughkeepsie and stayed there for five nights, living off room service and vending machine pickings, watching my money run out. The trucker's words had reignited old fears that closed around me like a fist: Max's body dumped in the woods, covered in a thin film of snow for some shocked ground crewmember to uncover. Or, worse yet, Max alive, the shadow of a faceless villain looming above her.

Defeated by these visions, I called Gwen and told her I was on my way back; she and Nathan could expect me by the end of the week. I checked out of the hotel mid-afternoon and returned to a world made damp and shining by the April thaw. Ribbons of half-melted snow ran along either side of the two-lane county highway. While stopped for gas, I unzipped my jacket and let the breeze lift up and under my flimsy sweater. My life stretched out before me like so much highway, stripped of all familiar landmarks. No Rhonda. No Max. I heard my daughter scolding me for my self-pity. *Snap out of it, Mom!* This was exactly what she'd said when Rhonda, passed over for a promotion, had cried one night after work. And I shouted at Max—called her cruel and selfish—and she shouted back, and Rhonda kept crying, and no one ate dinner, and how was I to know this chaos was a kind of love I'd learn to miss?

I got back in my car. I was cold and sweating, feverish. That night, combing the streets of a small town in search of a place to sleep, I found my hitchhiker.

Her name was Angela. She had a square face framed by neat curls, skin pocked with acne, and a damp green backpack that drooped from her shoulders like a wilted vegetable. She wore jeans, an orange flannel, and galoshes—no coat—and said she was sixteen.

"Where you going?" she asked when I slowed to pick her up.

"Anywhere you want," I said.

She held me in her stare a moment. The headlights of the car gleamed in her eyes, which were dark brown, like Max's. Then she climbed into the passenger seat, shut the door, and gestured east, toward the first stars. "That way's as good as any, I guess."

We drove through most of the night, heading in the direction from which I'd just come. All fatigue had left me, as had any notions of returning to Washington. I was bursting with questions about the girl, but held back, wary of scaring her. For her part, Angela seemed entirely uninterested in why a middle-aged woman should take directions from a teenaged hitchhiker. "Let's go left," she said listlessly when I came to an intersection. Then, "How's about we try this way for a bit." Near daybreak, she fell asleep. I pulled into a side road next to a sodden field and chanced a few hours of sleep as well, curled against the window. When I woke, my joints had tightened like screws. Angela watched me over the fold of a sweatshirt she must have taken out of her bag to keep warm. Her lips were thin and chapped.

"Are we ever gonna get something to eat?"

"We can," I said, "if you're hungry."

"I gotta pee first."

She stepped out of the passenger side door. The midmorning sun made a bright sheen of the mist rising from the wet field. Out of the corner of my eye, I watched her yank down her blue jeans and squat. I knew I should have given her privacy, but I was terrified that if I let her slip from my sight altogether, she'd disappear.

We ate breakfast burritos at a Taco Bell in a traffic stop town about ten miles north. I plugged my phone charger into an outlet. There were five missed calls, all of them from Rhonda. I sent Gwen a quick text, telling her I'd changed my mind and decided to stay in Missouri a little longer after all. Angela finished her burrito and scraped up the last of the salsa with a corn chip. Her gaze drifted onto my face and hung there indifferently.

I said, "My name's Dahlia, Dahlia Mun, but you can call me Dee. Everyone does."

She nodded.

"I'm taking a cross-country road trip," I went on. "I'm an artist. A photographer. I photograph . . . barns. But I'd be happy to drop you off somewhere. Is there someplace you're trying to go?"

She shrugged. In the glare of the hanging lamp above our table, her promise began to fade. She struck me as a little stupid.

She pinched some chip morsels from the bottom of the paper carton and sprinkled them into her mouth. Salty crumbs rained into the collar of her sweatshirt. I was disappointed. I wanted her to be more like Max.

We drove the next three days, Angela offering directions at every crossroads. She never spoke, not even to ask for food. She seemed to trust that we'd stop before she got too hungry. Each evening, I shelled out money for a two-bed motel room. Angela took long showers that filled the bathroom with steam. She left toothpaste smears in the sink, puddles on the floor next to the tub. One night, I emerged from the bathroom to find her sprawled in bed, watching a police procedural. Sirens howled. Cops cracked puns over a body bag.

"Turn that off," I snapped.

She obeyed. The room dropped into silence. I felt my frustration coiling like a spring as I got into bed. I wanted to be patient with her. She was still my best chance at finding Max, and she was only a child. But for all her apathy, I sensed that Angela knew exactly where she wanted to go. Though we might wander eighty or ninety miles south, or cross the border into Vermont for the day, we always returned to the same looping Adirondack roads, as if drawn by a great magnet. The runaway restaurant was near. Angela, for her own selfish reasons, was keeping me from it. I thought she'd grown complacent, reluctant to surrender the personal chauffeur who provided her with free lodging and food.

All of that would end soon. Nineteen days into my road trip, my credit cards were maxed out. Everything else I had was tied up in a 401K. I stopped for gas at a Stewart's, watching the white numbers tick higher and higher with a curious low-grade panic. Angela had gone inside to use the restroom. I no longer worried about her running off. She was with me, I knew, until I did something to drive her away.

I took out my phone. Three more missed calls from Rhonda. In the car, Angela had glanced at the phone resting in the cup holder each time it rang, but did not ask who I was avoiding. Now I leaned against the filling station and waited for Rhonda to pick up.

"Dee?"

"I need to borrow some money," I said. Angela emerged from the Stewart's with a pint of ice cream. I wondered if she'd stolen it or if she'd had some cash on her all along.

"Where are you?" Rhonda asked.

"Some place called Long Lake."

"That's not far from me. You could be here in two hours."

"Look, if you can't help me out—"

"I can help you," said Rhonda. She sounded so calm and reasonable. "But you need to come to my place. That's the deal. You have my address."

She hung up. Angela stood by the passenger side door, sucking ice cream off a plastic spoon. She'd rotated through all the outfits in her backpack and was wearing the orange flannel again.

"Are we going somewhere?" she asked. It was the first thing she'd said to me since returning my halfhearted "good morning" six hours ago.

"I don't know," I said. "Are we?"

She stared at me. I got into the driver's seat. Angela joined me in the car, and we pulled back onto the road. Old snow patched the fields in gray. Everything dripped, the air too warm for winter, too cold for spring. I didn't ask her where she wanted to go. I plugged in the GPS, which was still programmed with Rhonda's address. The ice cream melted quickly. Angela brought the container to her lips and slurped the liquid mint chip like soup.

Rhonda was renting a small brown ranch house two miles from the university where she worked. I parked in the shared driveway and told Angela I'd be right back. The last shards of daylight sparkled through the trees. I rang the bell and stamped my sneakers on the rubber welcome mat, aware of how disheveled I looked, how unwashed.

Rhonda didn't look much better. In Tacoma, she'd been proud of her graying hair and styled it in beautiful waves. Now it hung slick and drab past her shoulders. Swaddled inside an enormous knit sweater, she appeared shrunken and shapeless. She held out her arms to me, and we embraced in the doorway. It was all so familiar. Had Max really run away? Had any time passed at all?

"What's this all about?" she asked. She hung my coat on a peg behind the door and led me into a warm kitchen that smelled like burning oil. "Are you in trouble?"

"No. I've just been traveling, you know. For therapy. I took time off work to clear my head. I wasn't paying attention to my expenses, is all."

"That doesn't sound like you."

"Well. I've changed. Haven't you?"

Rhonda said nothing. She was never a chatty person, and over the years I'd learned to decode her gestures and silences for their hidden meanings. But now I had no idea what she was thinking. She took a hissing kettle from the stove.

"Tea?"

"No thanks," I said. But she poured me a cup anyway, because I wanted some, and she knew it.

As we sat sipping our oolong, Rhonda asked about the house and the city, the people with whom she'd fallen out of touch. Her tone was cautious, but I found myself happy to talk about Tacoma. I realized I was homesick. I missed the grand white bulk of Mt. Rainier, the perfect temperature that rarely dropped below freezing. And I missed Rhonda. All these months, our daughter's absence had sat between us like a stone, but tonight it encircled us, pressing us close. We would never be able to replicate what we had before Max left, nor could we return to our twenties before she entered our lives. And yet I began to see a way for us to be together again. I wondered if Rhonda could sense it, too.

Caught up in the possibility, I forgot why I'd come in the first place, until I saw movement out of the corner of my eye and Angela slid into the room. She'd come through the front door without making a sound. Rhonda startled and dropped her teacup.

"I told you to stay in the car," I hissed.

"Is she here with you?" said Rhonda, looking from Angela to me and back again.

"It's cold." Angela shoved her hands in her pockets. Her galoshes leaked brown slush onto the floor.

"Dee, who is this girl?" asked Rhonda.

"She's just a hitchhiker I picked up. I'm giving her a ride to—" I couldn't say it. It was too humiliating.

Rhonda recovered quickly. She was the sort of person it was very hard to surprise. She directed Angela to take her chair while she added more water to the kettle. Angela stared at me hollowly across the table. She looked like she hadn't slept in days, but I'd heard her snoring each night in the motel room. Rhonda draped a sweater across the girl's shoulders, then poured hot tea into a mug. As Angela bowed her head and began to drink, I felt an old, giddy rage heating my insides. I was angry at Rhonda for fussing over a child who wasn't ours. I was angry at Angela for her naïve willingness to be cared for by a total stranger. And I was angry at myself for bringing us all together in this terrible pantomime of home.

"You really are stupid," I said. Rhonda looked up, but I was talking to Angela. "I told you I photograph barns. Do you know how many fucking barns we've passed? Have I stopped to take a picture of any of them? Jesus, Angela. You can't go around getting into cars with strangers! I could be a murderer. I could have a chopped-up body in the trunk. But you wouldn't know any of that, because you're too dumb to suspect a thing."

Angela lowered her mug, her expression grave. This was nothing like fighting with Max. There was no answering rage to bounce off of.

"I've been driving you around for four days," I said. "You say you don't have any place to go. Well, you better find one, and stay there, because you're not gonna make it on your own. You're too trusting. You're too fucking young. And the next person whose car you get into? They *are* gonna be a murderer. They're gonna take you into some pimp's house, or drive you into an empty field—"

"That's enough," said Rhonda. She looked stricken. I saw she was thinking of Max, too. I stopped speaking and raised my teacup to my lips with shaking hands. Angela continued to stare at me, and I thought with resignation that she hadn't heard a word I'd said. But I was wrong: After a moment, she stood and walked out of the room, galoshes squeaking. I hurried to follow, but by the time I reached the front door, it was hanging open.

"Dee, what is going *on*?" said Rhonda as I grabbed my coat.

"I have to go."

I raced into the yard. Full night had fallen. I glanced wildly from left to right. Behind me, Rhonda flicked on the outside lamp, and I saw a figure marching down the driveway.

"Angela—wait!"

I caught up to her at the road, panting, a stitch cutting into my side. She stood with her arms wrapped around herself. I tried to give her my coat, but she wouldn't take it.

"I didn't mean it," I said. "You're not stupid."

"Yeah you did. And you were right."

A car sped by, spraying wet pebbles around our ankles. I could sense Rhonda watching us from her door.

"At least let me take you somewhere," I said. "A police station or—maybe—" I didn't know how to finish the sentence. I realized, finally, that I had no idea where lost children went.

A slim white hook of moon hung above a distant field. It was so silent here. I wondered how Rhonda stood it. Angela rubbed her hands up and down her arms.

"Okay," she said at last. Relief rolled through me. I felt like I'd been handed a gift. We walked back to the car once more, got inside. "But not to the police," said Angela. She buckled her seat belt and leaned back, palms braced against her knees. "I know where I want to go."

We drove an hour south, then another twenty minutes east. We were the only travelers on the road. Mountains rose around us, two shades darker than the sky. The clouds cleared. Driving along a narrow highway, flush against a forest of giant evergreens, we faced a panoramic of stars.

"Wow," I said.

Angela murmured a noise of assent. She had entered an unknown address into the GPS. Its directions led us off the highway and into a rundown town that cradled a body of water, a lake or a pond. It was impossible to tell in the darkness how far it went. Even though I knew Max wouldn't be waiting at our destination, I still suffered a wave of nearly unbearable defeat when we pulled up in front of a blue house with a crumbling front porch: not a restaurant, but someone's home, the faint babble of a TV leaking into the night. I rested my forehead against the steering wheel. I knew now that this journey had been for nothing.

Angela stepped carefully over the porch's broken steps and knocked on the front door. I joined her. I didn't know what else to do. There was a pause as the TV cut out. The door opened, revealing a large middle-aged woman in a faded green nightgown who shared Angela's square face. Her eyes widened. She screamed: "Bob! Bob!" An impossibly loud voice, like a foghorn in that quiet. She stepped forward and yanked Angela into a hug so fierce, it was nearly violent. "Oh, Angie. Oh, merciful God . . ."

A short man in a bathrobe came hurtling down the stairs. "What is it? What's going on?" He had his arms held to his chest, ready for a fight, but they dropped and hung at his sides when he saw Angela clasped to the woman's chest. "Angie," he said weakly. "Is it really you?"

The girl was passed inside to Bob, who held her more gently. The woman swiped her streaming eyes with the back of her hand. It was startling when she turned to me. I had forgotten she could see me. I had forgotten I could be seen.

"You're with the police?"

I shook my head. I didn't know how to explain. Inside, Angela buried her face in the man's shoulder. She leaned against him, exhausted. I could just make out her whispered chant: "I'm sorry. I'm sorry. I'm sorry."

NIGHT SHIFT

THESE DAYS, ISABELLE'S EXHAUSTION anchors itself in strange places. She feels it in her sagging wrists and the top of her head. As warm static at her fingertips. An oil slick in the gut. She's been the night attendant at the Speedway for seven and a half years. Never before has daytime sleep eluded her with such persistence.

What's changed? Nothing: Not the thickness of her blackout curtains. Not the quality of her pink foam earplugs. Not the volume of the neighbors who rent the apartment downstairs (retired couple, birdwatchers, porch full of wind chimes and prayer flags). Yet at noon, Isabelle invariably finds herself lying in bed as a tiny marching band blasts its horns between her ears. Or as old, idiotic riddles cartwheel through her brain on repeat.

What has four eyes but can't see?

Mississippi!

What can you catch but not throw?

A cold!

Her daughter, Lynn, recommends yoga and meditation. But what does she know? Lynn is an attorney for a makeup company called All Natural Beauty that recently came under fire for testing its products on guinea pigs. ("*Allegedly* testing," Lynn snarls whenever Isabelle mentions the lawsuit). She carries her stress like a war banner. Her back is a pretzel of knots. It's a point of pride with her that she inherited Victor's mania for long hours. "Daddy was *such* a hard worker," she commented the last time Isabelle visited for lunch, and Isabelle stabbed her fork into her salad and wished, as usual, that she had not come.

The Speedway manager, Baran, recommends valerian root tea. "The ancient Greeks used it to relax," he says. "It smells like an asshole, but it does the trick." Baran stops by once a month during Isabelle's shift to "touch base" and confirm that the little red pepper spray canister remains intact and ready for action beneath the register. His idea, not hers. Baran is twenty-six and feels bad about leaving an old woman defenseless.

After he leaves, Isabelle slouches forward and rests her cheek on the counter, inhaling the smell of Lysol. She likes the night shift— its mystery, its quiet. She likes how glossy and promising the snack packages look beneath the white fluorescence, so much so that she suffers a sense of letdown when she walks back to her car each dawn. Always she thinks there will be more mystery. *More* promise. When Baran drops by, she wants celestial fireworks and angelic fanfare to mark this glorious union between the forces of Labor and Management. Instead, she gets a discussion about asshole tea. Why would she want her mouth to smell like an asshole? Anyway, she needs something a lot harder than ancient Greek flowers. One of those tranquilizer darts they use on escaped animals at the zoo would be good. A sharp prick in the butt, a rubbery heat spreading to her fingers and toes, and she would be out for hours.

The bell jingles as the door flies open. Isabelle stays where she is, watching impassively as a kid in glasses and cargo pants hurries past the glowing wall of beverages. At the counter he halts, panting. A white triangular stud gleams in his left ear. His T-shirt reads: Tacos for President.

"I need ten dollars' worth of gas. Number four."

Isabelle sighs. Her breath makes a little smog on the Formica. With great effort, she lifts herself off the counter and prods the register awake.

"Thing is," says the kid. He grimaces. "I don't *have* ten dollars."

She blinks at him and drums her fingers.

"Look." He lowers into a kind of half-squat so they're eye to eye. "I ran out of the house without my wallet. Please? It's an emergency. My wife's going into labor and I—"

"Try again," says Isabelle.

He pauses. "My little brother got into a car accident and I've got to get to the hospital before—"

"EHHHH," says Isabelle, mimicking a buzzer. "You can do better than that."

He looks flustered. "I don't know what you want to hear."

"How about the truth?"

The kid jiggles his leg, and the keys clipped to his belt sway and jangle. He could be nineteen, twenty. "I think my boyfriend's cheating on me," he blurts at last. "Tyler texted that he saw him coming out of a bar with some girl."

"Well if Tyler said it," remarks Isabelle, "it must be true."

He seems not to hear. He licks his lips, patches of which are bright red and fresh-looking as though he picked at them on the drive over. "I just gotta know, you know? I gotta see for myself. I thought I'd try and get over there as fast as I could and catch them in the act."

"Then what?"

His forehead crinkles. "Well I—I hadn't really gotten that far. But I'll think of something. I'll know what to do. Please." The frantic, beseeching expression returns. "You can have whatever you want. My watch—" He sets it on the counter, a clunky digital thing, the inside of the leather strap faded from age and sweat. He begins to empty his many pockets. A crushed piece of Trident gum. A baggie with three green pills. A rubber band. The spring from a broken pen. A wad of tissues. Another rubber band. "You can have it all. I've *got* to get over there. My gas light's been on since yesterday. There's no way I'll make it without—"

"What are these?" asks Isabelle, nudging the baggie of pills with her fingertip.

He looks shifty. "Vitamins."

Isabelle considers the mess of him scattered across the countertop, everything he can afford to give. "All right. You leave all this here as collateral, I'll let you fill the tank. Then you come back once your quest has ended. Pay what you owe. Our transaction will be complete."

She taps the register again. The kid looks a little dazed, as if he can't believe his paltry bargaining actually worked. He runs out of the building without saying thank you. Isabelle watches him fill the old Ford. She doesn't suppose she'll ever see him again. The register will come up ten dollars short, but Baran will find someone else to blame. Phil the gawky teenager. Or Danica, who comes in to replace Isabelle at dawn.

She resumes her slouch across the counter. Around one, a taxi driver comes in for change. Then an exhausted-looking girl in pink scrubs, blonde hair a frizzy halo, purchases a pack of cigarettes and a diet Coke. Isabelle mops the floor. She eats her lunch: a plastic cube of Kroger potato salad and a raspberry Snapple snatched from the back of one of the refrigerators. It's quarter to three. The kid hasn't returned. She claws around under the counter for his baggie of pills, takes one, pops it into her mouth, and washes it down with a swallow of tea.

She waits for something to happen.

She and Victor used to get stoned when Lynn was at summer camp, but it's been a long time. She goes to make the coffee, wobbling a little on the still-damp floors. She divorced Victor when he cheated on her twice—first with their real estate agent and then with the high school librarian. Later, he got pancreatic cancer, and she had to endure Lynn's dewy-eyed proclamations of how *brave* he was, right up until he died in a bed at Bethesda North.

The coffee steams and hisses. Isabelle sips from her cup too quickly, and the liquid brings tears to her eyes. She never got to catch Victor in the act. The first time he came out and told her. The second time she guessed, and he didn't deny it. He was bizarrely honorable like that. No excuses, no entreating her to take him back, not even when he was dying and the librarian had abandoned him for a healthy man.

If she *had* caught him in the act? Isabelle tries to imagine her response. Crying? Hurling shoes and picture frames? No: She's always been too dignified to admit when she's hurt.

The floors are dry now. Still she continues to wobble. Her thighs feel like they're eight miles from her feet. She can't figure out how to bend her knees. Through a series of awkward lurches, she makes it back behind the register. She's so thirsty. The fluorescent lights emit a low organ melody. How has she never noticed it before? She closes her eyes, just for a second. When she wakes up, she's lying on the floor, and a tiny green dragon hovers above her navel, its wings beating a shimmering blur like a hummingbird's.

"Oh boo hoo," says the dragon. "Poor Isabelle. Poor you. So lonely. So cold. No one's got it harder than Isabelle. Lowest of the low."

She touches the back of her head to ensure she didn't crack it. Everything seems to be in order. She sits up. The dragon settles on the edge of the countertop, peering down at her through glittering purple eyes.

"Who are you?" asks Isabelle.

"Take away my first letter," says the dragon. "And I remain the same. Take away my last letter, and I'm still the same. Even take away the letter in my middle, and I won't know the difference. Who am I?"

Isabelle thinks for a moment. "Empty," she says. "You're Empty."

"No, you are." The dragon cackles. It's a sound of destruction, like pages ripped from a book. Isabelle shuts her eyes again, but when she opens them the dragon's still there, flying in tight circles around the rack of lighters and gum.

"I have a stomach," says Isabelle. "I have intestines and blood and lungs and bones—"

"You know that's not what I mean."

She does know. But she doesn't want to face it: the cavernous waste that finds her sweaty and sleepless at midday, that tempts her to its lip with its siren song of *regret, regret, regret.*

The door opens. A boy trots inside and yanks a six-pack of Dos Equis from the fridge. He's almost certainly too young to be buying beer, but Isabelle rings him up without carding him. She no longer hears the organ melody. She can't hear much of anything. It's as though her head's been packed with steel wool. It takes all her concentration to navigate the register's touch screen. The boy flashes her a grin and races outside to his truck. Isabelle sees a girl in the passenger seat with a long ponytail.

The dragon floats to the window and shakes his tiny head in disgust. "Young love is so uninspiring."

"I never said that," says Isabelle.

"I'm saying it right now, Crazypants! They don't know what's waiting for them. Abandonment, dejection. Or, if they're really unlucky, they'll get the long slow melt toward hatred."

"I didn't hate Victor."

"No. You loved him. You used to sneak out to the hospital and feed him ice chips at night. Never told Lynn, though, did you? Far better to go on acting vengeful and wronged. You know she's never forgiven you for how you treated him at the end. Her daddy dearest, Papa of the Year . . ."

"What can you easily break," says Isabelle, "but never touch?" She's desperate to make the dragon shut up and has the feeling that if she can stump him with a really tough one, he'll go away.

The dragon cackles again. "That's easy. A promise."

"What three letters change a girl into a woman?"

"Age."

"Everybody is attracted to me and everybody falls for me. What am I?"

"Oh puh-*leeze*," says the dragon. "At *least* give me a challenge. You're gravity."

Isabelle feels feverish. She stumbles to the nearest refrigerator, grabs a bottle of water, and untwists the cap. Her blurry reflection hovers over the colorful ranks of beverages. The dragon no longer speaks, but she can still hear him. *Mama*, goes the voice inside her head. It's the voice of an aggrieved eight-year-old: Lynn, begging for a Wonder Woman comic at the bookstore, though as the word repeats—*Mama Mama Mama*—it becomes untethered from its origin, and Isabelle realizes her daughter could be asking for any number of things she never received.

After the divorce, Isabelle cut herself off from the world. She drew Lynn into her self-exile. Wouldn't let her stay after school or go out with friends. Forbade sleepovers, birthday parties, home-coming, prom. They lived like filthy hermits, takeout containers crowding the arms of the sofa. The TV was always on, even when Isabelle stopped paying the cable bill and the screen glowed a harsh blue. That was the start of all Lynn's neuroses. She threw herself into her studies. She picked at her eyebrows and chewed the ends of her hair. Crescents of shed fingernails gathered beneath the kitchen table. The only reason she survived those years, Isabelle knew, was the weekends she spent with her father. Victor of the normal house and steady job. Victor, who went on doling out child support and alimony, never saying a single word against Isabelle, never threatening to take away custody, even though Lynn must have complained and he could see the yard falling into ruin, the wisteria vines snaking over the windows and sealing the house in darkness.

It is this silence that Isabelle resents the most. He was too polite, and she was too proud, and Lynn had suffered from their refusal to just have it out with each other, get angry, throw shoes. It's twenty years later, and she and Lynn still can't step outside their perfunctory script. They talk about groceries, politics, the weather, Lynn's job. Isabelle had always thought time would ease things between them. She sees now it has only frozen them back there before that glowing blue screen.

Isabelle sinks to the floor with her back to the cold refrigerator door, but it feels more like flying, like a giant hand has bundled her into a slingshot, drawn back the leather pocket, and sent her wheeling and flailing toward some unimaginable target.

"Hey," says the dragon. "Hey. Lady. Hello?"

It's not the dragon. It's Tacos for President. He's crouched next to her, waving in front of her face. Isabelle slaps his hand away. Her eyeballs feel like they've outgrown their sockets. The kid takes hold of her arm and helps her to her feet. Outside, the parking lot fills with the weird gray light of almost-dawn. An enormous crow perches on the ice bin. Isabelle staggers to the counter and leans against it. She flexes her fingers, curls them slowly and deliberately into a fist.

"Lady, you are high as all fuck," declares the kid.

"I saw a tiny dragon," Isabelle admits.

"Oh, him. He's the worst. Here." He hands her a crumpled ten-dollar bill. Isabelle smoothes it against the counter and presses it flat against her cheek.

"Your quest?" she asks.

The kid shuffles his sneakers. "Nick was sleeping when I got there. Alone. He'd just got off the late shift at Walmart. Turns out Tyler's sort of a liar. I guess he's, like, jealous of me or something?"

Isabelle slips the ten into the register and blearily counts out the drawer. She's having trouble with the numbers. She keeps looking around for the dragon. She can feel herself coming down, a sick settling like a dirty bottle sinking to the bottom of a pond. The crow in the parking lot caws once, twice. The door jingles, and Danica waltzes into the building clutching a purple thermos. She's in her late thirties, a dreamy girl with heavy wood jewelry and big headphones that she slides down around her neck. She asks Isabelle how her shift went.

"Usual," says Isabelle. She's afraid if she utters one more word she might throw up. She shuts the cash drawer. On a whim, she sweeps the baggie of pills and the rest of the kid's stuff into her purse. She lost track of him while struggling with the drawer, but she finds him in the parking lot, sitting on the hood of the Ford with his heels propped on the bumper, looking shiny and unspoiled in the day's first light.

"You got someone to drive you home?"

"I'll manage," says Isabelle.

"You shouldn't drive in your state. Let me take you."

She studies his features, the lines of muscle standing out on his young arms, and her thoughts leap briefly to the pepper spray taped under the counter. But she's tired and sick and for the first time in a long time, she doesn't want to be alone.

The sun rises above the highway. Cars clutter the on-ramp for the morning commute. It strikes Isabelle as miraculous that there are people whose days are just beginning. She feels like she's been awake for years. Air blasts through the rolled-down windows, smelling of hot tar. The passenger seat is pulled way back to accommodate legs much longer than Isabelle's. She can't remember the last time she was a passenger, but there's a sweet comfort in allowing herself to be driven.

One of her bird-watching neighbors sits in a lawn chair facing the woods when they reach Isabelle's apartment. He waves a pair of binoculars at Isabelle as the kid helps her out of the car.

"You just missed the most remarkable tanager!"

"Darn," says the kid. He leads Isabelle up the stairs to her door, whispering, "What's a tanager?"

"Bird," grunts Isabelle. She fits the key into its lock. "Why are you being so nice to me?"

"They were my pills."

"You didn't force them down my throat."

He follows her inside. She doesn't protest. A monstrous exhaustion is creeping over her. She stops at the kitchen sink to guzzle more water. The kid turns in a circle, taking it all in: the booklets of expired coupons taped to the fridge, the dead oregano plant on the windowsill, the pantry's scuffed accordion door, the years' worth of crusted noodles and scrambled eggs jammed in the groove between counter and stove.

"It's nice," he says.

"You're joking."

"Nicer than my place."

"I moved here after I lost the house. Child support ran out when Lynn turned twenty-one." She slips, nearly falls, but the kid's got the timing of some action movie hero. Together they amble down the hall to the bedroom. "Started taking these jobs," mutters Isabelle. "Cashier. Car wash. Parking garage."

"You like cars?"

"I like being around folks who are on their way."

She lands on the bed without drawing back the covers. The kid stands by the window. Light splinters the top of the curtains, covering him in bright splotches as he sways on his feet. The wave of her exhaustion crests. It waits to crash over her head. Isabelle extracts her purse from underneath her. She fumbles for his belongings and sets them one by one on the bed. He returns everything to his pockets, taking equal care with the pills and rubber bands and tissues, as though they are all precious mementos.

"You'll be all right once you get some sleep," he says. "You'll probably have a headache when you wake up. You got something for pain?"

"Why do you do it?" asks Isabelle. "Why do you take those pills when he says such awful things?"

"Usually I only take a half." The kid gnaws his lower lip. "I guess it's like, there's this little voice inside my head, hating on all the wrong things I've ever done. But the pills—they take it all outside me, where I can look at it. Fight it if I want."

Isabelle curls onto her side, smothering her laughter in a pillow. She wants to ask this child what he could possibly know about regret. She wants to present to him the unsolvable riddle of love and resentment that have curdled until one is indistinguishable from the other. But she also wants to find him here when she wakes. His stupid T-shirt. His ludicrous faith.

OTHERS LIKE YOU

IT'S THE HEIGHT OF tourist season in Barrett Beach, and the air thickens with the reek of new magic. I can smell it from the patio of the Captain's Lodge where I scrape seagull shit off the glass-topped tables. I can smell it inside as I stuff toilet paper rolls into cabinets and bundle bedding into the laundry cart. The hair lifts off the back of my neck and I salivate like crazy, a bizarre mix of dread and desire that can only signal one thing: There's a newcomer to our little town, and she's behaving badly.

Charlotte calls an emergency Congress. We meet in the basement of Open Sesame, Heather's locksmith store, on a rainy Thursday evening. It's always raining here at night, a warm, thin drizzle that worms down collars and makes the pavement steam. You'd think with a dozen witches in town, someone would be able to do something about this, but our powers have limits. We can't heal serious illness or reanimate the dead. We can't generate desired items out of thin air. As much as we might want to, we can't cast spells on other witches. If we could, I'd go for Charlotte, who appointed herself leader after Anne's death and clings to this scrap of authority with so much gusto, sometimes I think she's glad to have Anne gone.

"Karina Clayborne is the type of witch who gives witches a bad name," begins Charlotte, glaring around at all of us beneath her crooked bangs. She's already delivered the orientation packet and community guidelines to our latest arrival, a twenty-one-year-old from Arizona, but it hasn't stopped Karina from casting a muting spell on her next-door neighbor's Pomeranian, or a spell of changing on the mail carrier, transforming his postal uniform into a sexy nurse costume. I tug on the rim of my Tigers cap to conceal a smile, and Barbara coughs a laugh into her fist, but the others are uneasy. It hasn't yet been a year since Anne cast her love spell and our whole fragile world came unraveled.

"It smells awful," whispers Vicky, twisting her fingers in her lap. At seventy, she's the oldest of our group, and the least well-adjusted to our entrapment here at Barrett. Sometimes anxiety overwhelms her, and she won't leave her apartment for a week. Fatima, the kindest, brings her groceries from the Safeway, and Leela, the cruelest, wonders why we don't just let her waste away. "I can hardly stand it. All that bad magic polluting the air like car exhaust—"

"I enjoy the smell of car exhaust," remarks Heather.

"The issue isn't the smell," says Rei, rolling her eyes. "It's the threat of exposure. We developed these rules for a reason. Do we really want another Elliott situation on our hands?"

"Ladies, ladies!" Charlotte smacks the talking wand against the leg of her folding chair. It's just a foot-long stick wrapped in a shiny substance that might be aluminum foil. I never speak at these things, so I can't be sure. "What I would like to propose," says Charlotte, "is that we send a congressional emissary to *firmly* remind Karina of the regulations outlined in her orientation packet, and the penalties imposed for violating said regulations . . ."

"Why doesn't Sophie do it?" Sara suggests.

I tip up my ball cap and take in the whole of the room for the first time since sitting. Twelve women in rickety metal chairs. Twelve women who ought to be thirteen. We have the look of a support group, but our expressions are all wrong. Irritated. Fearful. Aggressively bored. "What?" I say. "Why me?"

"Sara, you are *not* holding the talking wand," chides Charlotte.

The stick is passed from hand to hand until it reaches Sara. I take back what I said before: On my list of people to curse if I could, Sara ranks number one. When I first arrived in Barrett Beach, I was struck by her lion's mane of red hair and her mouthful of bright, crooked teeth. Maybe I even flirted with her once or twice. By the time I caught onto her mean, gossipy streak, she'd already gone to Anne, citing concerns that my *carnal preferences* might distract me from congressional responsibilities. Anne told her to get a goddamn life and stay out of mine.

Now Sara wrings the talking wand in her fists like a wet rag and repeats her suggestion. "Sophie's closest to Karina's age. They can bond over their . . . common interests." Her voice lilts mockingly. She smiles, revealing all five hundred of her teeth.

Leela snatches the talking wand from Sara. "I second that. I think Sophie would be a great emissary."

I dive for the stick, but it's already traveling back around the circle to Charlotte.

"A motion has been raised, and seconded. We will now open it up to a vote. All those in favor of having Sophia Galanis serve as the congressional emissary to our newest arrival?" Charlotte lifts the wand like a conductor's baton. Ten arms shoot into the air. I slump in my seat and spend the rest of the meeting throwing dark, futile looks at everyone.

It's only later as I'm lying in bed, listening to a couple of the cats nose through my hamper, that I realize I should've bargained. I should've said I'd go admonish Karina only if someone agreed to take my night at Elliott's. I can't stand being in that house with him, spooning yogurt into his mouth, stuffing his limp, hairy legs into boxers. Imagining those legs wrapped around Anne's waist always raises a bitter taste in the back of my throat. I wish I were a better person. I wish Anne were here to visit Karina herself, as she visited me two years ago when I first arrived in Barrett Beach, nineteen and terrified, hiding in a motel room I'd magicked my way into without understanding how.

"There are others," Anne had explained. She'd appeared at the door with a paper carton of takeout wings—American code for I come in peace, she'd joked—and we sat on the motel's off-white carpet sucking hot sauce from our fingers. "You should join the Congress. We meet Monday nights." She slipped a chicken bone back in the greasy carton. Something about this gesture, its oddly placed delicacy, reminded me of my mother, who would have been about Anne's age if she were still alive.

"Yeah. Okay," I said. "I'll think about it?" I was still jittery and disbelieving. Only a few hours ago, I had driven to the edge of town and thrown myself against the place where the air condensed into an unseen wall, sealing us in. But I already knew I'd be going to the Congress. I would've done anything Anne said. A calmness emanated from her, something trustworthy and wise, almost sensory, like a soothing note hummed just below the level of hearing. And she had the most amazing eyes. Green-gold, like the sky before a tornado. I imagine Elliott looking into those eyes. I imagine he would've loved her, willingly, all on his own, if she'd given him the chance.

Randy is not happy when I tell him I need to leave the lodge early the next day, but I'm determined to catch Karina at work where it'll be harder for her to avoid me.

"It's peak season," he says, like I haven't noticed, like I haven't been washing sand out of bathtubs all month. As the Captain of the Captain's Lodge, Randy struts about the premises in full pirate regalia, doffing his tricorn to passersby and lobbing Elizabethan obscenities at the competing bed and breakfast next door. A year ago, I would've tossed an amnesia spell at him and been on my way. But I've grown cautious after Elliott. We all have. I wheedle and beg, make promises about overtime and kitchen duty while he joggles his big boot against the lobby's floor, enjoying the performance, and finally dismisses me with a wave of his stubby-nailed hand.

I've never been to the Pink Siren Diner before. The hostess seats me at a table in the corner, sticky with spilled lemonade. It's Saturday and the place is packed. Harried waitresses in sequined pink T-shirts, blue jeans, and half-aprons ferry steaming platters of fish fry from the kitchen. I know which one is Karina right away. Witches can always recognize each other, some sort of heat signature that rises from the body like a halo. We make eye contact over a table of men with matching sunglasses tans. Even with a heaping dish bin clutched to her middle, Karina stands straight-backed, arm muscles protruding as tight cords. Her hair is shaved to a brown fuzz, lips pursed into a pink pucker. The long-absent, hot-cold shock of desire pulses from my stomach to my feet.

She storms toward me, dishes rattling. Her eyes are large, brown, and pissed-off. Bright white stones stud the helixes of both ears.

"Why won't you freaks leave me alone?"

I glance down at the menu, playing for time. "I'll have the Reuben."

Karina glowers, like of all the ways I could've opened, this was the most offensive. She stalks back to the kitchen, the overlong apron strings dangling down the backs of her legs.

The lunch rush lasts another hour. Karina manages to ignore me the whole time. She marches between tables, collecting sticky forks and half-eaten burgers and sweeping crumbs into her palm with a damp rag. A child knocks a milkshake onto the floor. An older waitress with sweat stains down the sides of her pink T-shirt approaches me. "Have you been helped?"

"Oh, yes," I say.

She hurries off. I stare out at the windblown waves. In my imagination, the ocean promised all the possibility denied by my landlocked Midwestern childhood: fresh seafood, topless women in motorboats, cycles of newcomers each week so that no one stopped you in the street to ask after your mother's treatment, no one dropped off plastic-wrapped dinners like you and your stepfather were imbeciles who'd never learned to cook. I miss it now. I have dreams where I'm reborn into a child's body and get to do it all again—algebra and church picnics, corn mazes and scraped shins—but better this time. More lovingly. Like someone who knows it'll never last.

When I'm one of three customers left in the restaurant, Karina reappears. She clutches a turkey club and a pickle spear on a plastic plate, which she drops on the table in front of me.

"That's not a Reuben."

"Some asshole sent it back to the kitchen," says Karina.

"What's wrong with it?"

"Nothing. That's what made him an asshole."

I peel back the wheat bread to inspect the sandwich's contents. No hairs, toenails, or animal droppings that I can see. I lift the whole thing to my mouth and take a bite. This seems to please Karina. She slides into the booth opposite mine and plucks the pickle from the plate. There's a wet crunch when her teeth sink into it.

"I don't care what you say. I'm not going to your meetings."

"What meetings?" I ask.

"Don't play dumb. You get together and circle-jerk and do Satanic chanting in someone's basement. That chick with the bad haircut told me. Charlotte."

"Never heard of her." I take another bite of the sandwich. The lettuce is wilted, but it's not bad. Karina's mouth tenses. A drop of pickle juice dribbles from the corner of her lips.

"You're making fun of me."

"I would never."

A couple of waitresses lean on the counter, chatting, while a third rolls a yellow mop bucket toward the bathroom. Karina leans inward. There's a smudge of grease on her T-shirt between her breasts, and I imagine pressing my mouth to it. "I know you're one of them," she says. "I can tell. You stink of it."

"What?"

She struggles to get the word off her tongue. I sympathize. It'll clog you up like a mouthful of peanut butter, that word. But I want to hear her admit that she's felt the power slicking like hot oil beneath her skin. Her hands curl into fists. She leans closer. Is that an impending invitation I sense under the bristling fury?

"Magic," hisses Karina.

That evening she comes back to my apartment and we have sex, by which I mean, I bury my face between her legs for ten minutes and she sighs loudly—out of pleasure or boredom, it's unclear—and then we sit a long time on my sofa underneath an afghan, not saying anything, watching six or eight stray cats claw at the sliding glass door, their shadows spilling inside and flailing on the rug. Something about my powers calls them to me in droves. Sara thinks it's hilarious. No one else has this problem, and the things have proven immune to banishing spells. All I can do is let them inside where they blink contentedly, scratch themselves, and deposit the tiny half-eaten carcasses of rodents on my upholstery.

"I really can't stand cats," says Karina as they parade past her.

"Join the club." I shut the sliding glass door and flop back onto the sofa. Karina lifts a hand and sets it on my head. It's not exactly sexy, more like something you'd do to a dog, but I find myself relaxing under the weight.

"I hate it here," says Karina. "I hate the ocean."

"Not a lot of ocean in Arizona."

"I hated it there, too. I lived with my grandma. Most vile old bitch you could imagine. When I woke up one day with this idea to get in my Jeep and drive, just drive, I was so happy. Like, at last, I was gonna do something. I was gonna get the hell out."

I nod. I've heard this story before. We have all told this story before.

"Right around the Colorado border, I realized something was

wrong. I realized I wasn't driving. I was *being driven*. Like some crazy force had gotten hold of me." Her nails curl into my scalp. "The Jeep ran out of gas. It stopped in the middle of the highway. I sat and looked at the fuel gauge. Everything around me was dark. I thought, *what I really want more than anything in the world is for this motherfucker to start up again and take me where I need to go*. There was this click inside me, like a spark had lit up. I took my want and set it right on top of that spark. And then the car went. It started driving. I didn't need to steer. Didn't need to stop to eat or pee. Two days straight I drove. Until I hit this town. Right here."

I crane my neck to look at her, but I can't offer any answers. I don't know what force caused us to abandon our families and homes, what dumped us in this rainy coastal town and prevents us from leaving. Anne used to say we were being preserved for an act of greatness. Aliens would land on Barrett Beach, or a plague of locusts would darken the horizon, and there we'd stand, agents of salvation, the fate of the world resting on our shoulders.

"Listen," I say. "I know Charlotte's a dork and the Congress thing is totally overdone, but these meetings can actually be helpful. You can learn how to make a life here. You can meet others like you."

"I'm not like you. I'm not some freak."

"You've got a lot of nerve calling us freaks when *you* go around muting dogs and stripping mailmen your first month in town."

The cats are restless. Two tabbies scuffle by the fridge. A tortoiseshell with garbage strung along its whiskers leaps onto the coffee table and holds Karina in its steady orange gaze.

Karina has the good grace to look sullen. "How do you know about that?"

"Magic leaves traces. You'll start to notice once you know what to look for."

"I was only testing. I just wanted to know what I could do."

"We all do. But it can get us in trouble. There was an incident about six months back. People got hurt. That's why we need the rules. No taking money from people, no magic in public, no love spells. You don't follow the rules, you endanger everyone."

I wait for her to ask about the incident. I can't tell whether I dread or long for the chance to lay it all out, beginning to end, and ask for forgiveness in the telling. But it seems Karina's not listening. She stares into the parking lot, fingers toying with the zipper on the couch cushion. The tortoiseshell closes its eyes and purrs, a phlegmy noise like a clogged filter.

Karina falls asleep on my couch. I throw the afghan over her, and toss some shreds of deli meat on the kitchen floor for the cats. They converge on the feast. When I turn out the lights, their eyes glow like small moons.

We pooled all our cash to put Elliott up in a cheery blue bungalow a few miles inland where the tourists wouldn't bother him. Not that he's bothered by much these days. Abigail's chain-smoking on the porch swing when I arrive. She flicks a cigarette butt at me as I approach, and it sails a little too far, buoyed on a banishing spell that sends it arcing over the railing into the lawn.

"You're an hour and a half late. I called you three times."

"I had my phone off."

"He's sleeping now. I've done the hard part all by myself. You're welcome." She stands and stretches her arms so her denim jacket pulls up, revealing a swath of wrinkled brown belly. Abigail is the only member of our little group to claim that her life was improved by her powers, that the only things she left behind in Texas were an unlikable husband and several thousand dollars in gambling debt. Sometimes I'm jealous. Other times, I'm sure she's lying.

Inside, the house is warm and clean but frantically mismatched. Barbara insisted on fat pillows embroidered with corny messages about home and family. Charlotte bought a yellow clock that glows in the dark and whistles like a kettle on the hour. Gwen and Sara wanted a full-on beach theme—jars of seashells, potted palms, coat hooks shaped like anchors. Vicky filled the half bath with framed photos of '50s movie stars that Abigail keeps taking down because she doesn't like Debbie Reynolds watching her pee.

My contribution was humble enough: a rocking chair like the one my mother used to have, right down to its limp red cushion. I remember her happy in that chair, before the cancer, snipping coupons, reading *Little Critter* books to my brother. I settle into it, take out my phone, and begin to draft an email.

Dear Dad, how are you? Panama is beautiful as ever. Tomorrow we give a presentation on waterborne illness at the Ministry of Health. It's not as boring as it sounds. I'm getting along well with the other volunteers and even found one or two from the Midwest. This weekend we are hoping to have time to explore Casco Viejo. Has Justin filled out his college forms yet? Don't let him wiggle out of that. I know he's scared to leave home, but hey, I did it, right?

Love,

Sophie

I glance over the words. I shut my eyes and squeeze the phone in my fist to work on the spell, focusing on what I want him to feel: love, contentment, pride, a distinct lack of concern that he hasn't seen his daughter in close to two years. It's not easy, channeling such complex magic across computer networks. Many of the others prefer amnesia spells. They believe it's simpler, less cruel, to let their family and friends forget about them altogether. But I have to believe we're not bound to Barrett Beach forever. That one day this trap will snap open, and we'll erupt from its jaws like a charm of loosed finches.

I think I've got it now. Something close to what I need. This magic is so nebulous, so much like the weird logic of dreams. I open my eyes.

"Christ," I say. The word thuds in the silence like a dropped boot. Elliott is standing in the doorway. His gaze wanders the room, taking in the lace curtains and the television and the big brassy floor lamp and my body in the rocking chair as though it's all part of a dull and inscrutable art installation. Still, I'm spooked. The older women dote on him, escort him around town like he's a broken version of their own sons, but I've never been able to escape the feeling that he's faking it, biding his time, only waiting for the chance to take his revenge.

"What's the matter?" I stammer. "Couldn't sleep?"

He blinks twice, hard, as if trying to clear his vision. It's easy to see why Anne was attracted to him. Even sleep-rumpled, his face vacant as an empty bucket, Elliott is handsome. Silver threads his hair like glossy strands of Christmas tinsel. His eyes are deep-set glimmers beneath a heavy brow. I edge forward and suppress a shudder as I lay a hand on his arm. He lets himself be guided down the hallway to his king-sized bed with the memory foam pillows and Egyptian cotton sheets. How we spoil him, this man we've ruined.

Anne tried to keep him secret from us. She knew we'd smell the love spell on his skin and demand she reverse it. Turns out there is no reversing a love spell. The magic latches onto some existent kernel of mania, digs in deep like a parasite, and refuses to shake loose. Soon Elliott was weeping each time Anne tried to leave the house. He began following her, tormented by jealousy. I bumped into the pair in the frozen foods aisle at the grocery store one evening in November, the town steeped in snow and silence.

"Please don't tell the others," said Anne. "I know I can fix this. It's strong magic, but we're learning more about this stuff every day, right?" She gave a strained smile. Behind her, Elliott stood by the cart, kneading a bag of frozen peas and glaring at me. I could smell the magic steaming him like meat. For weeks we had scented this smokiness on the breeze, but we couldn't place its source. The prevailing theory was that Leela had fried her neighbor's subwoofer again. No one had dared to imagine this.

"Who is he, Anne?" I whispered.

"He's a carpenter. From Maryland. Came up in August to do some birdwatching."

"Jesus. And they haven't sent anyone looking for him?"

"I don't know, I don't know. I keep expecting . . . But maybe he didn't tell anyone where he was going?"

"Anne," Elliott said. "C'mon. Let's go home." I knew he was the injured party here, but the commanding edge to his voice made me want to smack those peas against his face until he choked out an apology.

Anne pressed my hand between both of hers. "Another week, Sophie. Two at the most. That's all I'm asking. It was a stupid mistake. Give me a little more time to make it right."

I couldn't believe she was begging—Anne, the strongest and most stable among us, the woman we trusted as matriarch of the volatile family we'd become. Unbidden, a memory surfaced: walking into my parents' bedroom, aged twelve, to find my mother at the bureau styling her wig on a mannequin head. She'd glanced up and made eye contact with me in the mirror. I'd never seen her without her wig before, and suddenly repulsed by the sight of her scalp, frail and shiny as a hard-boiled egg, I turned and fled down the hall.

I kept Anne's secret. At the next Congress meeting, I studied her for signs of unease, but she remained jovial as ever, laughing when Gwen rolled up her pant leg to reveal the scraped, stubbly effect of a botched hair removal spell. Those were happier days, when optimism came a little easier and we were filled with cautious intrigue about all that we could do. The Congress meeting after that, Elliott burst in on us midway through, wild-eyed and ranting:

"You can't have her! You can't have her!"

I believe that's what he screamed as he hurtled down the steps, diving at Anne like a rugby player. Thirty seconds: That's all it would've taken for Anne to explain. But in the panic of the moment, we reacted. Eight, ten, twelve spells hit him at once. Charlotte and I went with binding spells, Heather with a sleeping spell. Abigail, Leela, and Sara chose amnesia spells. We would sort all this out later, trying to untangle the magic one thread at a time while Elliott lay prostrate on the floor and Anne stood by, stricken, saying nothing.

Now Elliott frowns at the bed. It would be simple enough to hit him with a sleeping spell, but we've agreed not to use magic on him anymore. We hope that in time, the damage will fade. We have no way of knowing whether this is true. He plops down on the edge of the mattress, and I grab his feet and spin him around so he's reclining. I tuck the covers under his chin. He looks so much like a child. I'm glad I didn't tell Karina what happened. It will be good to have someone around who's untainted by the whole ordeal.

Half past eleven. I'll be here the whole night, but won't manage more than a fitful doze on the sofa. Fireflies gleam in the darkness beyond the living room window. I remember how, two weeks after my mother's funeral, my brother's dumb lizard got out and ate a dozen of them. We watched with helpless fascination as its frilled head quivered, its skin browned, and it wheezed for air. It was dead within the hour, and my brother, sick with rage and shame, forked its body into the river. We told my stepdad it ran away.

Karina appears on my patio, rapping her knuckles against the sliding glass door. She slips into the living room, a flurry of cats trailing her ankles like blown scarves. She strips out of her greasy pink T-shirt, sweaty blue jeans, sneakers, socks. Her underwear is sweetly, shockingly old-lady-like, baggy and bunching at the thighs. We have sex on the couch, never the bed. We speak little. Sometimes I wake from nightmares in which green creatures rise from the ocean, suckers pulsing on their bellies, to find her staring at me strangely, and I wonder if I've shouted something incriminating in my sleep. When I wake in the morning, she is always already gone. The cats lick themselves in patches of sunlight. I lie still, trying to reabsorb each detail. The jagged rhythm of muscles tensing and relaxing. The sudden nubs of her earrings beneath my tongue, small and cold as ice chips.

She still refuses to attend the weekly Congress. The others don't care. It's enough for them that her magical crimes have ceased.

"The air smells clean again!" declares Vicky, spreading her arms as though basking in a cleansing rain.

"As clean as it ever does around here," mutters Rei.

Charlotte waggles the talking wand. "I'd like to extend a formal thank you to Sophia Galanis for imparting a wise warning to our latest arrival." There's halfhearted applause. I grimace and tip the rim of my cap down over my eyes. I feel I've been tricked into caring for Karina so the others don't have to.

The usual business resumes. Gathered in our circle of folding chairs, we discuss our jobs: janitor, store clerk, exterminator, locksmith, these costumes we've donned to occupy time, blend in, move on. We share the new spells we've developed for hair loss and menstrual cramps, headaches and toothaches, spells to swiftly undo the tiny discomforts of a hangnail or bitten tongue.

"It's amazing how timid we've become," says Leela on our way out of the building. "The stuff we're capable of, and we're just gonna sit around healing stubbed toes?"

"What's amazing," says Abigail, "is that we haven't sworn off magic altogether after what we did."

"Hey—we're not *all* responsible for the vegetable, okay?" snaps Leela. "He was Anne's mistake."

They glare at one another in the glow of the lights outside Open Sesame. I smell the fury radiating from both of them, all the spells they'd like to fire at each other if they could.

September. The town softens on its slide toward autumn. Baffled seagulls strut the rims of empty garbage cans. Discount signs light the windows: 20% OFF T-SHIRTS! BUY TWO SCOOPS, GET THE THIRD FREE! Inside restaurants, bored hostesses tap lacquered fingernails against stacks of menus. The boardwalk falls so quiet, I can hear a broom rasping across the sidewalk three stores away.

Randy makes us stay late to give the house its end-of-season scrub-down. We hose the window screens and lay them in the grass to dry. We steam-clean the lobby floors and vacuum the sea-green curtains in each bedroom. We uncoil coat hangers and use them to fish wads of hair out of tub drains. Our staff is greatly diminished now that the college students have fled back to UD. The process takes all day. By the time I'm heading down the boardwalk, it's sunset, and the air feels misty and cool. An elderly couple trades a pair of binoculars, watching the last orange scales of daylight sparkle on the Atlantic. I'm grateful for the stillness but sad, too. The days ahead will be long and gray. Barbara will insist on placing a menorah in Elliott's kitchen. Gwen will decorate a plastic Christmas tree. Heather will joke that Elliott was probably an atheist, and somehow we'll get through it all again.

I smell Karina's Jeep before I see it waiting outside my apartment. The engine runs on stale magic. She hasn't filled the tank since leaving Arizona. She rolls down the window and beckons me inside.

"Where are we going?" I ask.

She doesn't answer. The car glides out of the parking lot as rain begins to fall. I realize I'm exhausted. My hips and back ache from bending and lifting furniture all day, and the tips of my fingers are sore from prying coat hangers apart.

Karina says, "I've been thinking about what you said."

"Which part?"

"How you can figure out where magic's been done by the stuff it leaves behind." She turns the wheel and we enter a side street overhung with holly trees. "A guy was sitting on the boardwalk yesterday as I was leaving work. One of your people was with him."

"Our people," I correct her. "You're one of us now."

Karina absorbs this challenge silently. "I could smell him right away," she continues. "He was burnt. Like something stuck to the stove." She glances at me. "I'm saying: I know what you did to him. What all of you did."

"It's no different from the shit you pulled with the mailman."
I'm surprised by my own anger. And of course, it *is* different.
Karina was testing her powers. We knew what we were capable
of. We made a choice: self-preservation. Given the chance, we'd
probably do it again.

"He was a creep, you know," says Karina.

"Who?"

"The mailman. He told me he liked my tight jeans, but that I'd
be prettier if I smiled."

I know what she's getting at. She would like to hear that Elliott
deserved it. Maybe he did. We know so little of the man he was
before arriving at Barrett Beach. Could the carpenter story have
been a serial killer's cover-up? Could he have been an evil person?
And would that have made it all right if he was?

I've realized where we're going. I feel the constriction that
happens when we approach the town limits. Karina stops at the
entrance to Route 1. Fields splay in the darkness on either side of
the headlights.

"I think my grandma might actually be worried about me."
She's not showing any signs, but I know she feels it too. Like
breathing through wet burlap.

"Send her a letter," I say. "Or an email. I can show you how
to stick a spell inside so she won't worry. She'll think you joined
the Peace Corps. She'll think you're saving the world."

The Jeep sits there, idling in the dark. I try to sense what other
spells Karina's done since I last saw her, but there's nothing. She's
empty—a shell scraped raw. She sets her foot on the gas pedal. The
Jeep crunches on gravel as it rolls forward. My chest tightens and my
lungs seize, and behind my eyes, a bright battery of fireworks erupts.
It's like slow electrocution, everything sizzling, preparing to pop.

Karina bends forward as if resisting a tremendous wind. "Isn't
there any way out of here?"

"No." My heart feels ready to detonate. "There's nothing.
Now would you back up?"

The car's doing it for her. It swings around and trundles fifty yards back the way we came. The air releases its grip on me. My eyeballs feel like two sponges squeezed of all moisture. Karina's slumped against the steering wheel. I reach out tentatively and set a hand on top of her head.

I could tell her about Anne's way out. About the ocean and the spell that weights you like an anchor. Even after we found her note, no one could believe it. For days we searched, certain she was buried beneath bed sheets in some motel room, counting cracks in the ceiling plaster, guilt-ridden and miserable, but alive. Finally I went to the shore. It was December, nighttime, holiday lights strung from all the beach houses. I waded in up to my waist. Icy water filled my boots, glued my jeans to my thighs. I went farther. My entire body rang with the shock of the cold. When the waves reached my chest, I felt it: the thrum of recent magic, like the echo of a gong. I stumbled back to the beach and lay beneath the stars, shivering. *You need to warm up*, I thought, and kept thinking it until I'd made it so, heat pushing through my skin as if through a furnace grate. I could tell Karina how my clothing steamed and how, watching the wreaths of white vapor drift skyward and vanish, I knew Anne was gone.

But I can't bring myself to speak of such things, not now, so soon after our failed escape. I suggest we head back into town and spend the night at the Captain's Lodge. The place will be spotless and empty. We can have our pick of bedrooms, share a bath, and wrap our bodies in fluffy pink robes.

Karina lifts herself from the steering wheel. "You want to pretend we're tourists?" she asks dryly.

And I do, yes, I'm not ashamed to admit it. Just this once, I want to play the role of newcomer. I want to be a person passing through, seeing this place for the first time.

PRESERVATION

FOR MANY YEARS AFTER I'd believe I periodically woke up, though the researchers assured me this was not the case. That the memories I retained—a shaggy dog laden with a tea tray, a voice crying out for more milk—were just figments of dream. I had been asleep the whole time.

As soon as the grogginess cleared, I asked for you by name.

"One thing at a time," said the woman aiming a flashlight into my eyes. Her breath smelled citrusy, and it struck me that I hadn't tasted a piece of fruit in over a year. "Can you get up for me? Slowly. That's a good girl."

The woman had me stand on my tiptoes, pace back and forth, and touch my fingertip to my nose. She recorded my height and weight on her clipboard. She asked me:

Did I remember my name?

Did I know what year it was?

Did I know *where* I was?

"Don't you think," I said, "I would be asking a lot more questions if I didn't know where I was?"

You were somewhere in this building. Maybe right on the other side of this wall. We had gone under together on January 11, 2015. We had slept through the beginnings of the refugee crisis. The nuclear deal with Iran. Another researcher would explain this to me later, offering a 2015 calendar with significant events marked in bold.

After changing into a fresh pair of clothes, I was led into a room I recognized as the clinic's cafeteria. The room was crowded with other study participants and the family that had arrived to greet them. I had no family. All I had was you. At sixteen we had run away from our parents' neighboring apple farms after your brother found us kissing in a nest of rotten Honeycrisps. The cops dragged us back. A year later, we repeated our stunt. This time no one came looking.

You were the one who found the study. Something to do with coma patient care. Participants could earn up to six grand. We were broke, sharing a studio above a beauty salon. The acetone fumes made us giddy. What was one year of our lives, sacrificed in the name of science? Sliding the warmth of our legs together beneath the cool sheets, we speculated on how the world might be a better place when we woke. Marriage equality. Hover cars. Clean energy.

When I couldn't locate you in the cafeteria, I hailed a woman in a lab coat, who took me to an office where she consulted a computer and informed me the name Lily Wilson didn't appear on the study's list.

"That's impossible." Panic sat strangely in my belly after all those months of quiet repose. "She went through the preliminary testing with me. We came on the same day."

The woman frowned and began typing again. "Did you say you were family?"

"What does that matter?"

"The confidentiality agreement—"

"Please," I said. "Just tell me what happened."

There must have been something in my voice. A crack of desperation. A lilt that reminded her of her own daughter. She had no obligation to tell me. She could've maintained her silence, called security to haul me away shrieking, and I would be here,

Lily, eight years later, wondering still what they'd done to you. How they had managed to separate us, whose union had seemed unquestionable since the time we were tiny children.

The researchers had turned you down. They had done it to hundreds of other eager participants. We'd seen them stumping out of the clinic's lobby and had fluttered our fingers in farewell. You told me nothing of this. When you signed on for a new study—run by the same research center but riskier, more lucrative—you told me nothing of that, either. On January 10, 2015, you hugged me goodbye. I was already wearing the mint green polyester pajamas. Then you went to the research compound next door for your own prep. The study was on cryonics. Extended live-body preservation. Most participants had signed on for one to two years. You had put yourself down for ten.

Lily, I am twenty-seven now. Studies like ours have become popular. Advertisements plaster the subways in colorful squares. Broke high schoolers go under to pay for college. Gamblers sleep away their debts. Protesters gather outside every clinic, railing against the exploitation of the poor. On TV, politicians gather to debate the ethics. My wife is one of them. I like to mute the news show and imagine that her moving lips relay a silent message just for me. Her influence bought me what I have striven for these past eight years: an appointment with your body, sealed in winter behind glass. Your face is the face of a nineteen-year-old. The hair has been shaved from your scalp. The researchers rigged the tank that contains you with a set of speakers, through which they occasionally blast opera music. Part of the study, I'm told. To see what the wakened brain might recall.

If I scrutinize your face for days, maybe I'll know why you did it. A memory will surface: I'll recall some comment you made over dinner about your exhaustion, your fear that the world was tipping into hate, your desire to put the years away like a cursed heirloom on a high shelf. But I don't have days. I have minutes, and your cold features are giving nothing away.

So I decide to speak. If you're dreaming, and if my voice has any influence over those dreams, I want them to be sweet. I tell you that nuclear weapons have been eliminated. That every refugee has found a home. That we have hover cars that run on clean energy. You should see them after sundown: how they sector the night into bands of dazzling brightness and the darkness that falls between.

WHAT DO YOU DREAM?

THEY'VE BEEN DATING AROUND four months when Neil begins dreaming Marla's dreams. All the shining wreckage of her childhood scatters itself through his sleeping hours. He wanders the Tulsa ranch house where she grew up, bow-tied teddy bears cackling from high shelves. He watches as her mother—dead ten years now, breast cancer—glides from room to room on a pair of old-fashioned roller skates. He sees Marla's old teachers, college roommates, ex-boyfriends, childhood neighbors, the half-brother with the mouthful of spotted teeth who never calls. He explores the dream-addled version of the office where she copyedits textbooks (quicksand in every cubicle, tentacles swaying from the ceiling like birthday streamers). He looks on helplessly as the small white bunny rabbit named Pancakes, which Marla had loved as a girl, flops down the driveway toward its death beneath the wheels of her father's Ford Taurus.

"Pancakes was a brown bunny, not white," says Marla when Neil recounts this dream fragment over breakfast. "Why would you name a white bunny Pancakes? That doesn't make any sense."

"I don't know what to tell you," says Neil. He finds himself saying this a lot around Marla, who remains just as mysterious to him now as she was on their first date.

In some ways, Marla is reliably boring, like Neil. She has a boring job, and a large square face that is unremarkable except for her wide-set blue eyes. Sex with Marla is consistent and undemanding. She gets off quickly, without much fanfare. After, she usually wants him to bring her something salty to eat, like Fritos or Pringles. She devours these snacks in bed with a palm cupped under her chin to catch any crumbs, though when she's finished, she dusts off her hands and the crumbs fly everywhere. Her diet is normal, which is to say, not very good.

In other ways, though, Marla is completely bonkers. From each paycheck, she sets aside twenty dollars to go toward her marble collection. They arrive in tiny square cartons from all around the world. Marla stores them in a jewelry box with a velvet divot for each one, and Neil isn't allowed to touch them. And her hair! It's so long she can wrap herself in it like a trench coat. She looks like one of those fanatical Christian women on TLC.

Strangest of all to Neil is the fact that Marla can apparently speak something like twelve languages. She has an insane gift for it. She picks up new dialects on a whim, the way other people pick up hats or shoes. She'll scold and grumble in French, Arabic, Korean, German, Swahili. Does Neil believe she can actually speak this many languages? Is he absolutely certain she's not discharging rounds of gibberish in what is either a very drawn-out prank or a more vindictive exercise in belittling his intelligence? No, he's not certain. Not at all.

This dream business is just the latest in a long list of oddities Marla has brought into his otherwise unexceptional life. As he smears butter over a slab of burnt toast, Neil decides that he's going to accept it, because he would like to shape himself into the sort of boyfriend who is accepting of such things.

Marla, for her part, remains unimpressed by this new dimension of their relationship. "It happens with all the guys I date," she says, reaching past him for the sugar, and Neil tries hard not to wonder just how many guys that might be.

After breakfast, they go to the gym in Neil's apartment complex, a starving little suite of squeaky machines and mirrors smeared with greasy handprints. They're both trying to lose weight, though Neil suspects he's trying harder than Marla. He mounts an elliptical. She wanders from station to station as if sleep-walking—two reps on the shoulder press, four minutes on a bike. She never adjusts the resistance. She uses whatever settings remain from the last person, like some aerobic leech sponging up the remains of a stranger's successful workout.

Does he love her? Neil ponders this question as he puffs away on his elliptical, sweat burning his hairline. His parents would prefer he found someone more sociable, more grounded, more Asian, just *more* than Marla, who seems always to have one foot planted in the room with you and one foot somewhere else entirely: Narnia, or Never-never land, or wherever it is she goes when her face fogs over like a breathed-on window.

And yet. He is infatuated with her. He can just sit and watch as she rubs lotion into the flaking skin on her knuckles, or strains pasta over the sink. It takes almost nothing to turn his thoughts in her direction. At work, hovering over a pair of grossed-out high schoolers slicing into their fetal pig, he finds himself thinking fondly: *I wonder if Marla would like pork chops tonight.* When he drives, he always imagines she's in the passenger seat. He pays special attention to the things he thinks she would find interesting. A woman waiting at the bus stop with four balloon animals and no children. A squirrel that has been completely run over except for its tail, a stubborn poof that stands perfectly erect and flutters in the breeze.

Neil's sweaty neighbors have begun eyeing Marla as she meanders back and forth across the room. She wears embarrassingly clean, traffic cone-orange sneakers. Whenever she passes in front of the oscillating fan, her hair comes alive, thrashing like a nest of snakes. Neil is torn between wanting to reprimand the gawkers—it's a free country! If a woman wants to wander around the gym like a lost child, let her!—and wanting to bark at Marla to please just *pick* a station and stay there for more than five minutes.

He dreams himself inside Marla's body. Or maybe it's Marla inside his body. They stumble through jungles, playgrounds, nursing homes, construction sites, classrooms, dorm rooms, and restaurants. They spill down staircases and waterfalls. They sprint after buses and cruise ships they'll never reach—this monstrous Marla-Neil who speaks in a guttural voice that belongs to neither of them.

Sometimes Neil recognizes the scenes of the dreams in which he finds himself. But more often, he requires Marla's interpretation the following day.

"A castle," he recalls as he drives her to her office, "with a huge lawn full of cakes on platters. Water in the distance. A guy in a tuxedo playing the violin."

"Oh, that must be the hotel where Meg's sister got married," says Marla, rummaging through her giant purse for sunglasses. "I've never been, but she said it was like a fortress."

Or he'll say:

"There was this woman? Pearl necklace? Teeth falling out of her head?"

"Aunt Fern," Marla informs him. "She always wears these huge fake pearls. I don't know why her teeth are falling out. She has perfectly good teeth."

For every setting or figure she can identify, there are a dozen Marla can't tease out. Neil finds himself frustrated by this. These are the dregs of Marla's days, the lingering ghosts of her childhood. If she can't shed light on them, who can? He presses her. She tells him to fuck off. They're having sex less and less these days, though in some bizarre tradeoff, they attend more events together as a couple. He brings her to the student vs. faculty bowling night. Over the clatter of struck pins and the whoops of over-caffeinated teens, he introduces Marla as his *partner*, because it sounds more serious than *girlfriend*, though he can't hear the word without a cowboy twang. *Howdy pard-ner. This is my pard-ner, Marla.*

She drags him to her company's holiday party. The publishing house has rented the back room of a popular Italian restaurant. Platters of shrimp, zucchini blossoms, and garlic bread cover the tables. Little plush elf toys sprawl across the rafters and perch on windowsills. The effect is supposed to be festive, but Neil only feels surveilled by their manic, glossy eyes.

Marla introduces him to a few people near the door—she says *boyfriend*—then promptly abandons him. It feels vengeful, though he can't imagine what he's done to deserve it.

At the bar he orders a beer, then two more. He's a bit nervous around all these book people, most of whom are older than him, married, and white. He finds himself talking to a pretty middle-aged woman with large breasts and red jingle-bell earrings. She says she had a dream about this party last night. It was just like this, really, except there was a giant bonfire eating through the floor. Every once in a while, a person would dive into the flames. There'd be a shower of gold sparks, like fireworks, and a smattering of applause.

"What do you think that means?" asks the woman.

"Social anxiety?" suggests Neil. He drinks deeply from his beer. "Last night I dreamed I was walking through Barnes and Noble when this man tried to kidnap me. The only way to escape him was to transform into different animals. I was a parrot, a swan, a mouse."

"How colorful!" cries the woman.

"It wasn't really my dream," Neil feels obliged to confess. "It was my partner's. Marla's. I only dream her dreams now."

The woman throws back her head and laughs, and her earrings jingle. Obviously she thinks he's lying, but she's enchanted all the same.

"Don't you miss having your own dreams?" she teases.

"Oh, no! My dreams were so—so *uncreative*. The night before a big test, I'd dream I had to take a big test. Stuff like that. If I even remembered them. Marla's dreams are so rich. Everything comes at me so intensely. Plus, I get to meet people in her life I never would've seen otherwise. Like her brother. He's this meth head. Lives out in Michigan. Total loser. But in dreams he's wonderful. He's always got a rope for me to climb when I'm stranded at the bottom of a cliff, or a laser gun to fight off the evil lizards . . ."

He feels a tug on his elbow. Marla, hauling him out to the patio where a group of smokers shivers in the glow of the outdoor lamps.

"You're making a fool out of yourself," says Marla. "You're making a fool out of me."

"I was just telling her a story."

"You're drunk."

"So?" He doesn't know why she's so upset. He sits down on the low stone wall encircling the patio and pats the spot next to him. Reluctantly, it seems, she joins him.

"I don't know why this dream stuff happens," she says. "I don't control it any more than you do. But it's not right to go around bragging. It's very self-serving." She takes the beer from where he's clamped it between his thighs and drains it in two gulps. He finds this sight oddly arousing and wishes, more than anything, that they were home in bed together, rolling through sheets full of Pringle crumbs.

The smokers finish and return inside. Neil's beery warmth has been replaced with a cold that saps all feeling from his extremities, but Marla appears unbothered. She's looking up at the restaurant's roof, drifting away from him in that way she does, jaw slack, hands limp and open at her sides. Searching for something to bring her back, he hears himself voice a question that he will later wonder how it possibly took him so long to ask:

"What do you dream? Do you see the same stuff I see, or is it all new?" An exciting thought occurring to him, he blurts, "Do you dream *my* dreams?" What a lovely balance this would be: each voyaging nightly into the forests of the other's mind, mapping all the roots and snares and dark, winding paths. But Marla shakes her head. She murmurs something under her breath in a language he doesn't recognize, but he can tell by her tone it's an insult or a curse. *Small man. Fuck off. Stupid.*

"You really don't get it, do you?" she says. "I haven't dreamed in years."

They don't break up right away. They peter out over the next few weeks. They *lose steam*—a phrase a friend had once used to describe his failing marriage, and which had recollected for Neil the wheeze of his mother's old Saab as it struggled to turn over on cold mornings. One day shortly after New Year's, he's cleaning his apartment and realizes it has been completely scrubbed of Marla. She's taken her toothbrush and hair scrunchies, her face cream and razor, her deodorant and the extra set of clothes she used to keep in the bottom dresser drawer. Her fatty dessert-flavored yogurts have disappeared from his fridge.

He calls her. He feels like some sort of closure is in order. To her voicemail he says, "I guess we both knew it was coming. For what it's worth, I had fun. I hope you did, too." She does not call him back. Neil searches himself for feelings of loss, but finds only bafflement. Did he do something to drive her away? He sifts through his memory. All he can think of is their argument at the holiday party. But that had been nothing! That was stupid. A drunken little spat. (Well, *he* had been drunk. He tries to remember if Marla had also been drinking and decides that yes, she must have been).

He throws himself into midterm prep, crafting overly detailed review packets on cellular parts and functions. He says, "If I were in a band, it'd be called the Endoplasmic Reticulum," and his students gaze back at him dumbly, grimly. He resurrects his

OkCupid profile and goes on a date with a nervous Korean woman who breeds labradoodles out in the country. All he can talk about is his dreams, Marla's dreams, which have only grown sharper with time. Last night, the amalgam *Marla-Neil* had stormed through a blinding tundra, pursued by dancing women in purple sports bras. Neil awoke from this vision sweaty and disoriented with items strewn around his bed. Pens and spoons. Hangers. The salt shaker shaped like a baying wolf.

"I teach my students that dreaming is a process of memory consolidation," he says as the waiter appears with their entrees. "Or else it's just an epiphenomenon to sleep. A random response to the electrical activity of the cortex. But the way I've been dreaming lately—it's hard not to feel it's something much bigger than all that. Like I'm receiving messages. Like I've been chosen. You probably think I'm totally crazy."

The dog breeder cuts into her steak and offers him a weak smile that says yes, she thinks he's totally crazy.

"Last week I had a dream two of my dogs got out," she says. "I crossed oceans looking for them, but it turns out they were in my old piano teacher's house the whole time. I think I have the ability to will happy endings out of my dreams, to circumvent the truly awful situations." She gives him a significant look, and Neil wonders dimly whether he's been labeled an Awful Situation to circumvent, or one out of which she might yet wring a forcibly happy ending.

But truthfully, he doesn't care. He's hardly listening. He's thinking of Marla with a belated sorrow that floods him so thoroughly, he wishes only to slip beneath the tablecloth and curl in a ball on the floor. Marla's purses. Marla's hair. Marla's half-assed makeup. Marla's palm full of marbles, their cream-and-peppermint swirls, how a boyish longing had risen within him to take those tiny, precious orbs to a steep place and scatter them down the incline.

Someday soon, he understands, *Marla-Neil* will scrape their way to the surface, plug their feet into his slippers, and carry him still groggy out the front door. He will wake in a place he doesn't recognize, a smear of bright lights dazzling him from above. Then all propriety will leave him. He'll break the breakup code. He'll call her just as soon as he can get his hands on a phone. "What does it mean?" he'll beg into her voicemail, and keep begging until the recording cuts him off.

RUNNERS

ERIN SAID TO TAKE only things that wouldn't be missed. An orange from an overcrowded fruit bowl. Two slices of bread from each loaf. A white nub of soap from the bathroom dish, a fresh bar already waiting to replace it.

That first house—a square brick home across from the middle school, ivy crawling over its face—I was jumpy and excited, thrilled by the ease with which the back door had given under my cousin's touch. Hadville, New York was the type of town where the neighbors all knew the names of each other's dogs and few people bothered with locks. It was so easy, strolling inside and helping ourselves to whatever we needed, that I imagined the house was a regular grocery store, except the owners loved us so much, they let us have everything for free.

I told Erin this and she laughed, the sound a pleasant melody in my ears. Erin had never laughed much when her dad, my Uncle Roy, was around. Now that he'd gone, she'd become a light-hearted version of the brooding teenager whose cold looks used to freeze me in my place.

"Why, here, have some broccoli, Miss Louise," she said, bowing and offering the green head in both hands.

"Why *thank* you, Miss Erin," I said, bowing back. "And would you like a can of our superb tomato soup?"

"Why thank you . . ."

We went on like that for a bit, until the noise of the house resettling scared us and we bolted. Then the long walk back to Uncle Roy's truck, which Erin had parked on a side street. She only had her learner's permit, but she was the best driver I'd ever seen. In all ways, Erin seemed older than her sixteen years. Though she attended the high school across town, during the day I imagined us bound by an invisible line. When the teacher handed out the permission slip for the Geva Theatre field trip, I smiled, knowing how Erin would forge Uncle Roy's signature with a flourish. When the other sixth graders snickered at my sloppy clothing and called me *hunchback* and *dyke*, I imagined Erin's icy stare turning them to stone.

After we got back to Roy's house, I heated up the tomato soup in two mugs and Erin boiled the broccoli until it was soft. We worked in the white glow of the little light under the microwave. Erin said we needed to conserve energy—make Roy's money stretch as long as possible—so we tried to only have one lamp on at a time. We took two-minute showers. Sometimes we lit candles. I loved those nights the most, when the flickering shadows blurred the edges of the room and I could pretend Erin and I were the last people on earth.

Erin set the broccoli on the table. She handed me a steaming mug and raised her own into the air. In the semi-darkness she looked queenly, hair cascading around her shoulders, eyes brilliant and unblinking. Before Erin, I had never known brown eyes could carry so much light.

"To our freedom," she said.

We clinked mugs and drank. The tomato soup scalded the roof of my mouth.

I had moved in with Erin and Roy after my dad, Roy's older brother, was killed by a delivery truck driver on the highway.

There was a settlement, and some money stashed away for me once I turned eighteen.

At first it wasn't surprising that my uncle had gone. Roy had disappeared before. Once when I was nine, and again last year before Christmas. He just ducked out, vanished for a day or two, and reappeared looking happy, or as happy as he ever did. In appearance, Roy resembled his brother—a small man with thin features and bristly black hair he tamed with gel each morning—but where the memory of my dad radiated warmth and laughter, Roy seemed somehow curled in on himself. Stunted. There was an ancient crabapple tree in the courtyard of Hadville Elementary that I had decided resembled my uncle: Both had the cramped, anxious appearance of creatures that hadn't seen enough sun.

He did make his efforts. He used to clap his hand on my shoulder in a brusque, brotherly sort of way—he never could seem to figure out whether it was all right to touch me, never kissed or hugged me like my father had—as he rattled off questions about school, trying to turn my one-word responses into fodder for more talk. He took me out to dinner, the best restaurants in town where the food came in tiny portions and the plates were ringed with bits of inedible green, or to the Little Theatre for artsy films I didn't understand.

Erin never came along on these trips. She and Roy had a coolly functional relationship that allowed little space for direct interaction. Erin cooked her own food and cut class as it suited her. Roy remained locked in his bedroom, which doubled as a home office, most of the day. Neither seemed to sleep much. In the middle of the night, I sometimes woke on the foldout couch in the living room to hear Erin returning from one of her walks, or Roy muttering on the phone. My uncle designed websites for a living. Some part of me believed these late-night calls were connected to his work, even as another part dreamily spun stories of exotic friends in different time zones, women with accents trilling my uncle's name.

Roy had kept a stern and spotless household, floors swept, shelves tidy, polished furniture arranged at right angles. In the weeks after his disappearance, the place acquired a lovely, lived-in feeling. Trash amassed in corners. Yellow stains blossomed on the counters and inside the kitchen sink. The yard grew unruly, spiky weeds poking through the grass. I'd been living with Erin and Roy for almost three years by that point. Now was the first time the place truly felt like a home.

Erin relocated to the master bedroom where her father had slept, and I vacated my foldout couch for Erin's bedroom down the hall. In the evenings, after we had both showered, I liked to sit on the edge of my uncle's queen-sized mattress and watch her comb her long hair. It was slick dark hair, almost black, like my dad's and Roy's. I knew my tan curls had come from my mother, though I'd never met her. She was gone before I started forming memories, and my dad, when asked, only distracted me with goofy stories about Mom growing fins and moving into the sea. A similar fate seemed to have ensnared Erin's mom, of whom there was not a single photograph in Roy's house. Perhaps this was why, in the beginning at least, I didn't make a fuss over my uncle's absence. Ours was a family where people simply disappeared.

Cold droplets spattered my arm as the plastic comb whipped through Erin's wet hair.

"How's our funds?" I asked. I didn't really care—I believed Erin and I could go on living like this forever—but the question made me feel important.

Erin hooked a bare foot around the handle of the metal suitcase beneath Roy's bed and drew it out onto the floor. "See for yourself."

I knelt and lifted the suitcase's heavy lid. Stacks and stacks of cash. Erin had found it on the fifth day of Roy's absence, when we were starting to run out of food. Fewer stacks remained now that she'd deposited some into her checking account at the credit union. She said it was crucial that we were able to pay the bills, or the bank would come calling. She said if we were careful, we could get by a long time on Roy's "emergency funds," to which he'd been stealthily adding for years. The problem was we didn't have much left over for food or other daily necessities. That's when we turned to people's houses.

"I'll take another chunk to the bank tomorrow," said Erin, setting the comb on the bed. "And the rest next month. You've gotta do it like that, in little bits, so they don't notice."

"We should take a vacation." I lifted one of the stacks and fanned it, smelling the ink. "We should go to the beach." I pictured the pair of us spread out on lawn chairs, baking gently in the sun. Dad had taken me to the beach once or twice. The Jersey Shore, it must've been. The era when I lived with my dad was generally a blur, but certain images stood out, the way pieces of a dream remain distinct in daylight. I saw a stretch of water, impossibly vast, umbrellas sprouting from the earth like giant cartoon mushrooms. I felt Dad's fingers around my own, and the wet squish of sand underfoot.

"Are you listening to me?" Erin reached down and rapped on my forehead with her knuckles. "Is anybody home in there? Didn't I just say we have to avoid attracting notice?"

"Yes," I said, blushing. I closed the lid and pushed the suitcase back beneath the bed. "I heard you."

The more houses we entered, the more comfortable we became. Soon we were strolling freely through unfamiliar rooms, no longer bothering to avoid windows or tiptoe across the floors. Messy homes were always good runs. Their pantries were crammed with so much expired junk, it was easy to snatch items without creating noticeable gaps, and we learned to identify these goldmines from the outside. They were the ones with blinds askew in the front windows, children's toys and bicycles sprawled in the uncut grass.

It seems odd to me now that Erin wanted to rob homes when

stealing from a store would have been so much safer. If you were caught with a bag of unpaid groceries, you could always claim you zoned out and forgot to pay. There were no excuses for getting caught inside someone's house. I think she must have enjoyed the invasions. As we scavenged, she brought me odd artifacts—cutesy magnets in the shapes of US states, wooden knickknacks, beaded keychains, paperweights with morphed flowers in their cores— never to take, but to remark over with mutual amusement before returning to their designated place. She delighted in the randomness, the colorful sprawl that Roy had never permitted to gather in his home.

But photographs were her specialty. She liked to remove the backs of the frames and flip through the pictures that had accumulated over the years.

"Look," she said, splaying the photos like playing cards. I saw a dark-haired young woman in a black cap and gown, a grinning girl with braces, a skinny child of five or six on a bicycle, and an infant with a red face squeezed into a scowl: the same girl, I understood, passing through time. Glancing from right to left, she aged. Left to right, she shrunk.

My own preferences were different. While Erin roamed living areas and kitchens, I marched into master bedrooms and threw open closet doors. I'd begun to note my body's changes—the way it curved and bulged as other girls' bodies did not. Suddenly, my toes bunched at the front of my sneakers. Shirts rode tight across the chest.

I'd never tried on women's clothing before, though I often imagined what my mother might have worn. I put her in cool colors, mostly, to accent the dark blue eyes I remembered from the one portrait of her I'd seen. The day I first donned a stranger's dress and heels, I played it like a joke, grinning cheesily as I shed jeans and an old sweatshirt of Erin's that was already too small.

I gazed at my reflection in the full-length mirror. The dress, spun of green sequins, hung loose around the middle, but across the bust and shoulders it embraced me perfectly. I swished side to side, and the skirt twinkled. I hiked the dress in one hand, used the other to push my hair behind my ears. A stranger stared slyly back at me. Her eyes were stern and secretive. Her legs, taut above the high heels and covered in a soft down, looked beautiful and strong.

I rooted around the closet until I discovered a silver cross for my neck, and gaudy rings for all my fingers, and earrings that appeared crystal but were really glass, which I dangled beneath my unpierced earlobes. My whole body shimmered, as if covered in bright scales. I was so overly decorated it made me laugh. I'd never seen myself laughing before. I laughed and laughed, loving how it lifted my cheeks, how it tightened my belly into a board.

Erin didn't share my affinity for these items. My cousin dressed for camouflage. Dark T-shirts and cargo pants slung low on her skinny hips. I didn't hold this against her. Erin had the lean, bare beauty of a wildcat. Girlish accessories would have masked this, robbed her of something essential. But I needed new clothes, and I didn't want the rejected fabrics in the back of the closet, the worn-out blue jeans and T-shirts emblazoned with charity logos. I wanted the clothes I tried on. The skirts, blazers, and dresses. The blouses with their frills. I wanted the strappy sandals that encased my feet like little cages, and the pantyhose that turned my legs to silk.

That afternoon with the green dress, I hesitated. The days were warming. The bedroom smelled like stale sheets. I heard Erin calling softly to me from downstairs: "Lou? You ready to go?" Another of my cousin's rules: Never linger longer than twenty minutes. Suddenly embarrassed at the prospect of discovery, I stripped off the dress and stuffed the jewelry back in its drawers. But the heels I placed carefully in my backpack.

I told myself Erin would understand, once I took the time to explain myself. This woman wouldn't possibly miss a solitary pair of shoes. Even if she did, she would attribute the absence to clumsy misplacement, not thieves. But when we got back to Roy's house and unloaded our bags, I chickened out. I made sure to keep my backpack tilted away from Erin, so she couldn't see into the bottom.

One afternoon in early May, a man showed up at the door. He was not the first adult to appear on the front stoop since Roy left. There was a mother with some Girl Scouts, and a woman from the VVA asking for clothing donations. This man didn't hold a clipboard or a package. He was bald, with large crooked ears, and he thrust his whole head into the hallway when Erin told him Roy wasn't home.

"Not home?" His eyes lingered for a second on me, standing in the kitchen doorway with my fists clenched. A warm breeze flowed into the house, carrying the scents of cut grass and exhaust. "Isn't that his truck in the driveway?"

"Someone picked him up," said Erin.

"Who?"

"*I* don't know." She was playing the uninterested teenager and doing a good job at it. Only someone who knew her well could pick up on the tension in her shoulders. "He never tells us when he's coming back. He's real thoughtful like that."

The man squinted. I took a few steps closer, wanting nothing so much as for him to lunge forward and shove my cousin out of the way, and then I would be on him, biting and kicking. A car sped by, windows blazing in the sun. At the Sunoco across the road, someone was setting orange cones in a semicircle around the pump.

The man rocked back on his heels and smiled. "I work with your daddy. Company sent me to make sure he was all right, seeing as we haven't heard from him in a while."

"What company?" Erin said. "Do you have a card I can give him?"

His smile flickered. "He'll know the number. Just tell him Mike stopped by. When he gets back. Tell him to give Mike a call." He turned and stalked toward his white car parked at the end of the driveway. It stayed there the rest of the day and into the evening. Erin's bedroom faced the front of the house. I turned off all the lights, lifted a slat in the blinds, and stood there watching until my legs ached and the car finally pulled away.

It was about 9:00 p.m. Erin sat in Roy's bed, reading what looked like a textbook. She never cared much for school, but now she had to keep up her grades so she didn't give the administration any reason to call in Roy for a meeting.

I still trusted my cousin, yet the encounter with the stranger had unsettled me. It had thrown a shadow, like a long arm, over my uncle's disappearance. I thought of the cash in the suitcase, the late night calls. For the first time, it occurred to me that something really terrible might have happened to Roy.

My cousin set her textbook aside. "Can I help you with something?" There was a challenge in her stare. I shuffled my feet against the floorboards.

"I was just wondering—" Erin's lips tightened. I felt a door swinging shut between us, realized then that by living this life with her, there were questions I'd implicitly agreed not to ask. At the last moment, the words changed their shape in my mouth: "I was just wondering whether you knew—what happened to your mom."

Erin had been so unfriendly in the days before her father left that I'd never thought to ask this question. Now anticipation prickled my skin. If I couldn't know what happened to Roy, perhaps solving this mystery would suffice. One explanation in place of the other. I could tell the question surprised Erin. Her fingertip traced a pattern on the cover of the textbook. "Not really." She frowned. "Roy used to tell me that the women in this family were runners. They had the itch. They'd hear a call, and they'd be off . . ."

Her gaze drifted to the window where the long blackout curtains shivered in the breeze. She paused as if listening. I tried to listen, too. I heard the roar of traffic, someone yelling at the gas station, and music pulsing from inside a building or a car.

"D'you think he could've been talking about my mom as well?" I asked softly.

Erin's eyes snapped back to me. "How should I know? I didn't even know I had a cousin until we got the call about your dad." She reopened her textbook. I realized our moment, if I could call it that, had ended.

I was at the doorway when my cousin spoke again.

"Anyway, it doesn't matter where they went. What matters is they're gone, and they're never coming back."

Not everyone in our community was equally trusting. Sometimes Erin and I came to houses whose doors were locked. In the early days, this was enough to send us off in search of easier takings. But as the weeks passed, Erin became bolder. She showed me how to pick a lock with a torque wrench she'd pocketed from Home Depot. She instructed me to make a step out of my interlaced fingers and heft her up to the low roof above a back porch. Though she was five years older, we were now nearly the same weight, and she was better at crawling along shingles to reach an unlocked window on a second floor.

There were close calls. On a Monday afternoon, I met Erin in the middle school parking lot the second classes ended at 2:20. It was always safer to break in during school and work hours when people left their homes, but in this house we found a man snoring on a couch in the dark living room, a muted TV throwing light across his face. Erin took me by the hand and we backed out slowly, slowly, the way we'd come.

Another time, a woman came home while I was still in her bedroom, trying on her clothes. It had become a habit by that point. Dresses, sweaters, blazers and skirts, pants suits and scarves and shawls and hats—I coveted them all. I heard the door slam, heard her call out to the mutt who'd greeted us enthusiastically fifteen minutes before. Under cover of the dog's long nails clattering against the linoleum, I sneaked down the steps and out the front door. It banged shut behind me, and I ran, not looking back, tripping over the woman's long skirt, the paisley fabric catching at roots and burdock as I sprinted through the woods that led to the side street where Erin had parked Roy's truck.

She was already in the driver's seat.

"Why didn't you get me?" I panted, hoisting myself into the passenger's side.

"What was I supposed to do? Scream your name? What are you *wearing*?"

"It's just—it's a joke." I could feel my cheeks reddening. "I was gonna come down and show you."

"I don't think it's your color," Erin said.

My blush intensified. We drove home in silence. That night, instead of eating dinner with Erin, I stayed in the hall bathroom and scrubbed the stains out of the skirt using a dishrag smeared with detergent. I hung the skirt from my closet door and climbed into bed, drawing the covers up to my chin, though it was barely 7:00 p.m. Darkness fell slowly. I watched the skirt's paisley fade to an indeterminate gray, then black, listening to the scrape of cutlery from the kitchen. I expected Erin to stop by my room and apologize for leaving me. If the situation had been reversed, I knew I never would've deserted her.

But her light footsteps, when they sounded in the hallway outside, passed without stopping. This second abandonment stung worse than the first. The next house we broke into, I didn't hesitate: I took a blue minidress and a pair of black heels and stuffed them into my backpack. I brought these prizes home and displayed them, along with the paisley skirt, on the left side of my closet, segregated from the shapeless rags I wore to school each day.

Every night I played dress-up. Every night I spotted a new imperfection and sloughed it off: pimples popped, split ends trimmed. While Erin was doing homework in the kitchen, I snuck into the master bathroom in search of a razor. The drawers opened on a jumble of my uncle's possessions, which Erin must have cleared off the bathroom sink. I found a jar of his hair gel, opened it, and inhaled. The piney fragrance brought him back to me in such a rush, I had to sit on the bathtub ledge. Roy was really gone. I hadn't loved my uncle, I barely even knew him, but I realized his presence had been a protective barrier, keeping out something that now roamed through the house like a cold draft.

Eventually, I located a plastic razor in the medicine cabinet behind the mirror. Beside it was a sheaf of little papers, wrinkled by steam. They seemed out of place with the Band-Aids and bottles of pills, so I picked them up. Photographs, a dozen total. All captured children roughly the same age, between three and eight, I guessed, girls with brown hair and brown eyes and wild, wicked expressions of delight. I recognized the girl on the bicycle, as well as another of a toddler in a pumpkin costume, which Erin had shown me at a different house. I squeezed the stack until the glossy paper crinkled in my fist.

The man with the white car didn't return. May passed into June. Roy had been gone over two months, and it began to seem incredible no one missed him. Not a nosy neighbor, not the man who brought the mail. If I disappeared, who would worry about me? The school might send someone, but what if I vanished over summer vacation? Would Erin call the police?

Against my will, we were settling into the way life had been before Roy left. Erin and I no longer cooked together, or laughed or talked. I started to resent the sight of her dishes piling up in the sink, forks gummy with cheese, a fine brown crust burnt into the bottoms of Roy's steel pans. She resumed her nightly walks. I wondered if she was visiting high school boys who slid their palms into her back pockets and nested their chins in her hair. The thought made my stomach burn.

When we entered houses, we went our separate ways and reconvened twenty minutes later at the truck, so it was easy for me to take whatever I liked. To my expanding wardrobe I had added a skirt and blouse, a sweater, three more dresses, a pair of white sandals, a pair of leather boots, and a lacy white shawl. Some of these items fit better than others, or fit only in certain places, but I cherished them as if they'd been tailor-made. I loved the sleek watery feel of silk, the reassuring stiffness of starched cotton, the knitted grip of wool. When sandal straps bit into the backs of my heels, I learned to love the sting.

But I would never have risked wearing any of it outside my bedroom if it hadn't been for the pearls.

I discovered them inside a jewelry box beneath a fake velvet bottom that opened like a trapdoor. The house—a renovated Victorian near the mall—was the nicest place Erin and I had entered. There were deadbolts on all the doors to protect the flat screen TV, the antique furniture, the crystal vases stuffed with bamboo. Erin had to scale the ivy and go in through the second floor bathroom while I stood in the woods keeping watch. We thought there might be an alarm system, but it never went off.

In the master bedroom, I pinched the necklace between two fingers and slowly lifted, the strand of pearls unraveling with tiny clicks. They blushed with a hint of pink, chilly against my palm as if plucked from cool water. Jewelry hadn't really held my attention on previous raids. It seemed so impersonal, less like it was made special for me. But those pearls. I had never wanted something more.

I folded the necklace in toilet paper and placed it in the pocket of my backpack. I tried it on later at home, shivering when the pearls rested like cold fingertips against my throat. I would wear these, I knew, to the Geva Theatre field trip next week. I would wear them with the skirt and the blouse and the white sandals already stained rusty from my split-open blisters.

On the appointed Friday, I brought everything to school with me in a paper bag so Erin wouldn't see, and changed in the bathroom before we were loaded onto the bus that took us downtown. Some of the girls laughed when they saw me, but I didn't care. For the first time I felt strong, like the outside of me matched who I'd always wanted to be. The usher told me I looked smart. The teacher complimented my pearls and wanted to know where I'd gotten them.

"From my mom," I said. "She gives me lots of things."

And as soon as I said it, it seemed to be true. The lights dimmed. Actors walked on stage. For homework we had to write an essay analyzing their performance, and I would have nothing to put. I had spent the whole show fingering the pearls and thinking about Roy and my dad and Erin, too—their small hands and feet, narrow waists, slim shoulders—knowing, finally, that my shape was my mother's. The long torso, big feet, and growing breasts belonged to her.

Maybe the realization made me bolder, or maybe I'd been craving a confrontation with Erin all along: a shouting match to lift us from our painful silence. I didn't change clothes before taking the bus back to Roy's house. In the kitchen, my cousin stood before the lit microwave where a plate spun and spun. Dirty pots, cutlery, and glasses crowded the countertop. A spiral of fruit flies floated over two shriveled peaches and a blackened banana in the basket on the table.

"How could you have done this?" she said. "How could you be so stupid? Don't you understand what we have here? How lucky we are? You start getting greedy, and it's gone. Foster care. Locks on your door. People keeping track of where you go all the time. Is that what you want? To be a prisoner?"

Those were her words, but I think mostly she was mad that I'd gone behind her back. It didn't occur to me to point out the secret photo collection I'd discovered behind the bathroom mirror. My audacity had evaporated. I had never seen my cousin truly angry before. I trembled as sweat dampened the blouse under my arms. In that gloomy room with its stench of mold and garbage, I felt myself at the center of a terrible ruin that had been creeping in on us for weeks.

The microwave had gone dark, the reheated food forgotten. Erin swept out of the house without bothering to shut the door behind her.

That night, I set out on foot. It was raining, a light drizzle that felt like mist on the skin, but soon soaked my T-shirt and jeans. The stolen clothing I had packed into Roy's metal suitcase and slid underneath my bed. I envisioned burying it later, or heaving it dramatically over the High Falls. But the pearls were curled in my fist. If I could return them, I could take it all back. Erin would forgive me. It would be like none of it had ever happened.

It took over an hour to reach the house by the mall, perched like a great noble bird on its hill. For twenty minutes I stood in the wooded backyard, watching. Outdoor lights glared above the back porch, but there was no movement in the windows. I convinced myself the family must be out for dinner and a movie with friends. I believed it so deeply that even after the man sprang at me in the hallway with a baseball bat, pulling back just in time—"Jesus Christ, I almost killed a kid," he muttered over and over while his wife dialed 911—all that registered in my mind was confusion.

"I thought they were out of the house," I told the police-woman who drove me to the station. For hours, it was all they could get out of me. "They should've been out of the house."

At some point I must've coughed up my name and address, because Erin joined me at the police station later that same night. She sat straight-backed and silent in the little room with the coffee machine where they'd set us up, and I copied her, grateful that she was there and could show me what to do.

Even so, it didn't take long for the cops to work out that we were on our own. No one had heard from Roy in weeks. He'd missed his latest project deadline and the company figured he'd quit, such an oddball to begin with, just like him not to give any notice.

For a while the cops seemed to think Erin might've done away with Roy herself. They led me to a room with a bed to let me sleep, and the next day, a woman with square glasses drove me back to Roy's house so I could gather my belongings. But for Erin, they had many days of questions. Where had her father gone? Did she know about the gun he kept in the safe behind the closet? Did she really expect them to believe he'd dropped off the face of the earth?

I found all this out later. Erin didn't say a word to me in the station, still mad, I guess, that I'd gotten us caught. But once we separated, she seemed to forgive me, or maybe she was just lonely. She called me twice a week from the new facility where they'd moved her—"a little less than juvie, a little more than high school," she once described it. She said she was okay and making friends and stuff, but at the end of August, a week before I started at my new middle school, she ran away. She never mentioned her plans to me, but I was unsurprised when Laura, my foster mother, broke the news.

"I don't want you to worry. They're gonna find her," said Laura, squeezing my wrist in her warm fingers. I liked Laura, and her husband, but the pair of them didn't really understand me. And they certainly didn't understand Erin, if they thought she would ever let herself get locked up again.

After we finished talking, I went to my bedroom and shut the door. Laura's house had three floors, and my room sat high at the top. Wooden beams sloped from the middle of the ceiling to the base of the walls. The window overlooked the long driveway and the distant county road, along which the occasional car skated like a rolled marble. There was no roof beyond the window, not even a ledge to place a foot. Just a straight drop, thirty or thirty-five feet to prickly rose bushes and hard gray slabs of sidewalk.

I didn't want to run away. Not then. It was just a mental game I played, a daydream of scrolling countryside and wind whipping through my hair. It would be years, still, before the call came and I answered. By then they would've found Roy, living out west under a false name, eluding the people whose profits he'd been laundering until he got cold feet and fled. But not Erin. Not our mothers. I would follow their example. I would go where I couldn't be found.

That summer evening in Laura's home, I sat on the bed with the handmade quilt, content, tapping my toes against the floor and listening as echoes raced up the walls. The room remained mostly empty. From Roy's house I had taken only my toothbrush, some old clothes, and the photograph of the skinny girl on the bicycle. I told the social worker it was a picture of my cousin, and she believed me. If you weren't looking too closely, any of those photographs could've passed for Erin.

WONDER IN HER WAKE

IT WAS TEN O'CLOCK at night, and the doorbell rang again.

Dustin flipped onto his stomach and stretched his limbs until his hands and feet gripped the edges of the mattress. He stayed that way, stuck to the sheets like a barnacle, as the doorbell clanged five, six, seven, eight more times. The kid out there on the stoop must've had his finger pressed to the button. If Dustin were braver, he'd go barreling out there in his Avengers PJs, seize the prankster in both hands, and send him flying all the way to the mailbox with preternatural human strength. But Dustin wasn't brave. He'd known this about himself for as long as he could remember, as assuredly as he knew the flaky texture of his always-chapped lips or the pattern of freckles on his skinny arms. He was nine years old.

He hadn't been sleeping long, but as the doorbell's final note faded to silence, a terrible alertness blazed through him. He climbed out of bed. His room was dark except for the glow of the street lamp coming in through the window. Two months ago, someone had thrown a baseball that fractured the glass in a starburst pattern. Ever since, the light had a squished, lopsided quality as it fell through the splinters. He put on his slippers and walked down the front hall. He peeped through the curtains, but the stoop was empty now. In the kitchen, he found his mother sitting on the floor, her collection arrayed around her in a messy ring. Tiny animal bones, feathers, cool blue rocks, bottle caps, and strips of fabric Dustin had torn free from the wire fence encircling the dump.

"Couldn't sleep?" asked Frances.

Dustin shrugged. There was no point mentioning the doorbell. His mother had stopped hearing it, just as she'd stopped seeing the grocery store cashiers who grinned at each other when she came through the line with her bulk tubs of spices and rotten fruits. She beckoned to him. He joined her inside the ring, squatting with his arms folded on his knees.

"Once upon a time," said Frances, "there lived a shapeshifter with many names. To some she appeared as an old woman, to others as a raven or a moth. You might not know it was her in the moment, but you always recognized her after she'd gone by the sense of wonder she left in her wake."

Dustin rocked on his feet. Frances picked up a white feather and twirled it by the quill. She was fully dressed in blue jeans and a button-up speckled with tiny airplanes. Her body pushed against the fabrics when she moved. She was the biggest, tallest person Dustin knew, including their next-door neighbor Mr. Herman, a tree-cutter whom Dustin had once seen yank a dead sapling right out of the ground.

"One day the shapeshifter wanted to create something beautiful. She scooped up a feather from one corner of the universe, and the well-worn T-shirt of a little boy from the other. She folded the feather inside the T-shirt and buried it in her garden beneath a tree." Frances took a scrap of green cloth from her collection and demonstrated, wrapping it around the feather like a bandage. "She waited. A hundred thousand years went by. Then a hundred thousand more. The shapeshifter wasn't bored. She got to be all kinds of things during that time: a dinosaur, a sunflower, the snow on a mountain. Finally, she went back to the tree. There among the knotted roots sat a little boy with a perfect pair of silver wings. He was the loveliest creature she'd ever laid eyes on. The shapeshifter became a raven. Then she and the winged child flew across the universe together, looking for more things to create."

Frances returned the feather and the scrap of cloth to their designated spots in the ring. She smiled. She didn't tell her stories often. They were reserved for hushed, magical moments like tonight, when the house slipped beneath the surface of its silence and stayed there, holding its breath. Dustin thought of himself as collecting the stories the way Frances collected crumbs of dead or discarded life. Mentally, he gathered up the shapeshifter and the winged boy and added them to the display case alongside the cross-eyed wizards, talking cats, shy pixies, and invisible wolves of his mother's worlds.

"What do you say?" asked Frances. "Are you up for the challenge?" She gestured to the ring and Dustin, eager, leapt to his feet. He left the house through the back door. It shocked and thrilled him that his neighborhood was full of people sleeping in their beds, that he should be the only one to feel the cold grass springing beneath his feet. He climbed over fences, a sense of mystery tingling between his shoulder blades as he flitted from yard to dark yard. A dog growled and strained at the end of its chain. The breeze smelled like damp paper. The sky was clear, the moon full and round as a pearl. Dustin slid down the creek's banks and spread his fingers across the ground, looking for items that would please his mother. Heart-shaped pebbles. Shiny soda tabs. Flower petals crushed and leaking fragrance. "Garbage," Dustin's father used to say. "Why are you wasting your time with such garbage?" But he knew better than to mess with Frances's collection. He'd toss a chair across the room when he got really angry. He'd rip the screen door off its hinges. Never would he touch those jars packed with stray bits of beauty.

In school the next day, Dustin was so tired his head slumped onto his desk. Mrs. Blakemore clapped to wake him the way Mr.

Herman clapped to scare possums out of the garbage cans. His mother never tried to scare away anything. She never set traps smeared with peanut butter or sprayed poison along the base-boards. Their house teemed with scurrying. Mice skipped through the walls. A cat lived with her babies beneath the back porch. Dustin heard their mewling each morning when he ate his toast.

His classmates giggled as he roused himself and tried to focus on what the teacher was saying. A girl stuck out her tongue and twirled her finger around her ear in the sign for *crazy*, and a few others joined in while Mrs. Blakemore's back was turned. Last year he'd had a friend named Brianna, who saw his neat handwriting and asked him to do the captions for her cartoon dog comic strip. *Woof, Woof*, wrote Dustin. He didn't feel very clever, but Brianna shrieked with glee and they began eating their snacks together every day. Then she moved away. On her last day at school, she kissed Dustin's elbow and said she'd never forget him. He still wrote her name in the margins of his language arts notebook, big bubble letters that looped around the page.

He walked home from school slowly, passing ranks of ash trees with orange blobs spray-painted on their trunks, marking them for slaughter. Mr. Herman said the ash borers were good for business, said those tiny green beetles paid for his new furnace and the lease on his car. Dustin only felt sad looking at the doomed trees with their furrowed trunks and bald heads.

The closer he got to his house, the more the injustice welled up inside him. It was not fair that Brianna had moved away. It was not fair that the ash trees were dying. It was not fair for his mother to send him on midnight scavenger hunts that left him puffy with exhaustion the next day. Already he'd forgotten his willingness, the fantasy of wings unfurling from his back. His mother's magic was for nighttime and now it was day, the spring sunlight hard against his face.

At the creek, Dustin turned left and entered his neighbor-hood with its colorful clapboard homes. It was a straight shot to his house at the dead end, so he had time to observe the three girls before he reached them. They crouched behind Mr. Herman's heap of leftover firewood, backpacks grouped at their knees. The breeze carried their giggles down the street.

"Hey," said one of them as he walked by.

Dustin turned. These girls were older than him and wore the plaid green uniforms of St. Vincent's. The one who'd spoken had lots of blue makeup gunked around her eyes and her skirt hiked up around her knees to keep it from dragging on the sidewalk.

"You know who lives there?" She jerked a thumb in the direction of Dustin's house. In the gap between her legs he spied a triangle of purple underwear. The sight sucked all the air out of his body. He shook his head.

"I'm telling you, Mal—that's the one," insisted a pale girl with chubby arms. She pointed over the firewood to Dustin's front porch. "My cousin says it's got all those weird plants and her nasty old car in the driveway—"

"How about a crazy witch that lives around here?" Mal pressed. "You heard of her?"

"She killed her husband after he kicked one of her cats," offered the pale girl eagerly. "Put a curse on him so a big beam fell on his head at work . . . Now she just lives off the money from the factory, sitting inside all day, working on more spells."

Dustin shook his head again, mouth dry. "No, I don't know anyone like that."

"Let's go home. I don't want to get in trouble," said the last of the three girls, who had a square, sullen face and a long yellow braid that touched her tailbone. "What if we do the wrong one and it's like the mayor lives there, or a cop . . ."

"The mayor wouldn't live in a shithole like this."

"A cop, then."

They chewed on this possibility. Dustin wanted to leave, but felt frozen by the girls' impossible magnetism. He longed to reach out and wrap a hand around that rope of hair, or run a finger along

Mal's shining eyelid to collect its blue gloss. Mal looked at him, looking at her. "Let's make him go check."

She rose, grabbed Dustin by the shoulders, and yanked him into their conference. He felt the tingle of hot breath in his ear. He smelled the strawberries and honey and sweat wafting off their hair and clothes. Then he was marching on stiff legs toward his own door, feeling lightheaded and chosen, as though he'd spiraled into a dream.

Pots and hanging baskets cluttered Frances's front porch. Her plants seemed human in a way plants shouldn't—the pursed lips of their blossoms, the long blue fingers of fruit. Dustin had watched his mother murmuring into the flowers' nodding heads as she coated their leaves with water from a spray bottle. He rang the bell. It sounded small and lonely from out here, a gong struck on a rainy hilltop.

He didn't expect Frances to answer. She never went to the door when the neighbor kids played Ding-Dong-Ditch the Witch. But he lingered, curious. He wanted to know what it was everyone saw: why the adults shook their heads at his mother, why the kids played their pranks and the teenagers threw stuff at the house before speeding away in their cars, laughing. He wanted a rationale, something that would make Frances's oddities click satisfyingly into place like a key into a lock. He waited and waited. A figure approached through the window's mottled glass, shivering, enlarging. Fear scattered sudden needles in his chest. He realized he did not want to be on this side of the door, yet once again, he'd lost his ability to move. He waited. The plants puckered their lips. The door swung open, and Frances stared down at him. The flyaway gray hairs on the top of her head brushed the doorframe. Her button-down shirt was patterned with small black orbs—olives or eyeballs—and her arms hung at her sides like great stilled pendulums.

"Well," she said gravely. "Are you coming in?"

Now it was guilt slicking its hot trail through his belly. He knew he ought to go inside with his mother, but those girls were watching. He vaulted off the front porch, running so fast his backpack thudded against his bottom. "It's her!" he screamed. "It's the witch!" He didn't go back to Mal and her friends. He ran straight into the woods until the wet dirt muffled the sound of his footsteps, until the trees converged behind him and he could see nothing of the house.

He planned to keep going until he was tired, but he hadn't fully exhausted himself when he reached the dump. He poked his wrists through the diamonds of the wire fence and peered into the trash pit. It wasn't an official city dump. People just came here to throw out things they didn't want. There were musty couch cushions and mismatched sandals and greasy pool noodles and toaster ovens with dangling wires. Two years ago, someone found a finger. The police appeared and roped off the place with yellow tape. "That's it. That cesspool is over and done with, and good riddance," Dustin's teacher had said. She hoped they'd pave over the place and build a T.J. Maxx or a HomeGoods. But all that happened was the police left, and someone ripped down the tape, and people went right on dumping their dirty mattresses and broken stoves.

Teenagers liked to gather on the other side of the pit nearest the high school, smoking cigarettes and flicking the butts into the trash. But today there was only a fat, white-haired man stomping around, plucking items and dropping them into a garbage bag. Dustin found the section of cut-away fence, peeled it back like a curtain, and slid down the slope to watch. The man wore baggy brown pants covered in pockets and a sleeveless shirt that showed the white tufts under his arms. Loud music thumped from a pair of headphones. He bobbed his head and waggled his hips as he bent to retrieve a can. When he straightened up, his small brown eyes found Dustin. He wrenched the headphones down around his neck.

"Kid, you better skedaddle. This place is toxic."

"What are you listening to?"

"A classic!" The man offered the headphones. They were too large for Dustin's head. He pressed the pads against his ears to keep the headphones from springing apart. He listened to drums crashing, the snarl of what might've been a guitar. "What do you think?" asked the man as Dustin passed the headphones back.

"It's okay."

"What do you think it *sounds* like?"

"A monster?" Dustin guessed.

"You're a sharp boy. That's Metallica's "Call of Ktulu." You know what Cthulhu is? No? He's a big water monster, sometimes described as an octopus or a dragon . . ."

"Like a shapeshifter?"

"No. He's only got the one shape. It's just that people think of him in different ways, compare him to different things. You follow?"

Dustin sank onto his knees and scraped a fingernail through the crusty dirt. He was thinking of his mother now, wondering how long she'd watched his retreating back before shutting the door. He did not suppose she would ever tell him another story again.

The man sighed and fumbled in his pocket. The music cut out. "You in some kind of trouble, kid?"

"I made a mistake," said Dustin.

"Did it involve a girl?"

"Sort of, I guess."

"Well! That's nothing to be ashamed of. Hell, I'd be worried if you *weren't* making those kinds of mistakes. I wasn't much older than you when I started going around, breaking girls' hearts. I know you can't see it now, but I was a real looker, you follow? Nice thick hair, good teeth."

He sighed again. Dustin continued to draw ridges in the dirt like small mountains, or cats' ears. Mal's friend hadn't gotten her story right. Dustin's father hadn't kicked any cat. What he'd done was pick up his son and shake him until Dustin's teeth rattled in his head like dice. Dustin's memory got a little foggy after that. He remembered his mother shouting, his father laugh-crying. They made thunder when they fought, like gods, floors wobbling, frames crashing from the walls. And soon after, yes—the accident at the stamping factory, and a funeral service filled with gruff, solemn men who patted Dustin's shoulder and avoided his eyes. "He wasn't always cruel," Frances explained when they got back from the church. It was the only thing she ever said about his father after he'd gone: *He wasn't always cruel.* Like a person could wake up one day with a mean seed sprouting in his belly.

"Hey." The man nudged Dustin with the toe of his boot. His face was the color and texture of caked mud, and creased in a kind smile. "How'd you like to help me find some treasure?"

"What sort of treasure?"

He opened the bag so Dustin could look inside: bottles and cans thick with grime, some of them buckled with the imprint of a squeezing hand. "Just promise me you'll watch where you're going," said the man. "Don't step on any glass or needles. And don't touch anything. Just holler at me when you find something. All right?"

They spread out. Dustin kept a close watch on his sneakers as he lurched over the mountains of trash. He passed a boxy TV set, a graying pair of men's underwear flapping from the antenna. He stepped over a crumpled lampshade and a pair of binoculars with the lenses punched out. The smell of the dump was intense, like old cheese rotting in a drain, but Dustin felt happy. He was good at treasure hunts. A natural, his mother always said. Maybe he'd even find something here for her collection—a present to apologize for the way he'd run.

"Here!" he called, pointing at a dented can wedged between a mini-fridge and a legless patio chair. The man came running, the bag clanging over his shoulder.

"Here!" Dustin cried again, pointing to the green neck of a bottle peeking from a split garbage bag. He found so many that the man rescinded his rule and told Dustin to pick the items up himself. The bag grew fat from its plunder. Dirt and grease blackened Dustin's fingertips.

"That's quite the pair of eyes you've got," said the man as Dustin handed over another can. "You and me make a good team."

"Hey old man!" shouted a voice. "Hey, Santa Claus, up here!"

It was the teenagers from the high school, strung out along the far edge of the pit with their legs dangling. The sun, low now—Dustin realized it was almost dinnertime—hung over their shoulders and darkened them into silhouettes.

"Hey Santa, anyone ever tell you child labor's illegal?" The boy's voice cracked on the second syllable of *illegal*. Laughter followed. Someone threw something, a snack bag or candy wrapper, that fluttered into the pit and vanished among the piles.

The man shook his fist. "Anyone ever tell you to mind your damn business?"

One of the others said something in reply, too quiet to hear. More laughter. Dustin curled his dirty fingers into his palms. The man took a huge breath, held it for a moment, and released. "C'mon, kid. Let's see if we can find one or two more while the light's still good."

They spread out again. They stuck to the side closest to the woods, farthest from the teens, but the louder cries continued to reach them.

"Hey Santa! You so lonely you'll do one of your own elves?"

"Hey Santa—does Mrs. Claus know about this?"

Dustin wanted the man to shout at them again, but he'd replaced his headphones. The teenagers lit their cigarettes. Embers glowed from the shadows of their mouths. They began to yell at Dustin: "Hey kid, what's he paying you? We'll give you double if you yank those pants off his fat ass." Dustin's ears burned. He thought some of these kids might have rung his doorbell once or twice, or driven past the house late at night, honking. The thought was like a splinter between his eyes. He bent over to pry out a water bottle from under a rusted ironing board. Something whistled over his head and shattered.

The man ripped off his headphones and exploded into screams. "What in God's name is wrong with you? You could've taken off his fucking head. He's just a little kid, for Christ's—"

Another hurled projectile. More shattered glass. The man cursed. He and Dustin hurried up the side of the hill, through the fence, and into the woods.

"We're just trying to help you out!" yelled a boy. "C'mon, Santa, can't we help you build your toys?"

The bag had torn on the jagged edge of the fence. Dustin collected everything that had fallen free and brought it under the trees. The man dug inside one of his huge pockets. He pulled loose a second garbage bag and shook it out until it ballooned like a parachute.

"Stupid, arrogant little—if I were ten years younger—bunch of cowards . . ." He glared at Dustin. "You just gonna stand there, or you gonna help?"

Together they bundled the ripped bag into the new one. Dustin began to pile the spilled items inside. He stopped when he saw the picture on the bottle in his hand. Dirt had obliterated much of the label, but he could make out the faded image of a person crouched on a railing, a pair of wings arcing from their back.

"Gotta get these over to the recycling center by eight," muttered the man. "You got the time on you?" He reached for the bottle. Dustin twisted away.

"I want this."

"Quit goofing around."

"I helped you find all those bottles," insisted Dustin. "This is the one I want to keep."

The man scowled. "Well here's a little piece of life wisdom from me to you: *You don't always get what you want.* Hand it over."

Dustin clutched the bottle. The light shifted as it fell through the swaying treetops, brushing shadows across the man's face. A muscle in his cheek twitched, as though he were about to laugh. Then he lunged. Dustin dodged him, and they went around like that in tight circles, the new bag rolling and clinking as they knocked into it, the man grunting and cursing until he got tired and sat in the grass, chest heaving, sweat glimmering in the wrinkles on his neck. He made a visor out of his hand and squinted up at Dustin.

"Okay. All right. You've beaten me. You happy? Now get out of here."

Dustin didn't move. He wanted to explain his mother's story. The T-shirt. The feather. The boy and the shapeshifter. He didn't want another person disappointed in him today. He wrung the bottle in his fingers. The man got to his feet and leaned into Dustin's face. His breath smelled like the sweet must of old apples.

"*Go*," he said.

Dustin ran. The long straps of his backpack flicked against his sides. His arms pumped wildly. On each upswing, the empty bottle seemed to grow heavier, filling with air like a throat.

It was an hour at least until sunset, but the clouds rolled in and insects began to trill. The evening grew prematurely dark and cool. Dustin emerged from the woods, spent. His sneakers weighed a thousand pounds. He was hungry and very thirsty.

In his mother's gravel driveway, he stood a moment, trying to understand what he saw. The whole house moved and flailed like an animal in a trap. He approached cautiously, the bottle clenched in his fist. Something was *on* the house. He reached up to pinch a corner of the flapping substance between forefinger and thumb. Toilet paper. Rolls had been tossed onto the low roof where they unraveled, trailing past the windows and catching on the thorny bushes by the sidewalk. The front porch had mostly vanished beneath soft white heaps. Dustin set the bottle on the step and unveiled the plants one at a time. He thought he heard them sighing as they gratefully stretched their long necks.

The house lights were on. Dustin's mother had been inside the whole time, and done nothing. For a second he was so full of helpless rage, he would've hurled the bottle against the house if it had still been in his hand. He rested his forehead against the cold, shut door. He saw the years inflating him like helium, plumping his limbs, rounding out his chest. Whatever happened, he would never allow people to treat him like they did his mother or the Cthulhu man. He would become strong. A boy classmates skirted in the hallways. A boy who wandered the streets at night not on his mother's errands, but as a balm for the unhappy restlessness itching under his skin.

He jumped back as the door opened with its familiar soothing creak, and there stood Frances. A piano melody fluttered over her shoulders into the night. She only had two CDs, but by some subtle enchantment, Dustin never heard the same song twice.

Her face was in shadow, so he couldn't tell whether she was mad at him or not. When she extended her hand, he thought she wanted him to take it, even though he was much too old for that sort of thing. Then he remembered the bottle. He passed it to her and she lifted it up to the light. An anxious minute passed. Her other hand reached for him, and this time he didn't hesitate: He grabbed hold and let her lead him around the side of the house to the backyard.

The ash tree loomed large beside the dilapidated shed, one of the few in the neighborhood to have been spared the bite of Mr. Herman's chainsaw. Dustin laid a hand against the grooved trunk, imagining the noise of the larvae tunneling through the wood, though he couldn't hear or feel anything. The tree, against all odds, appeared to be in good health. Without asking, he knew what his mother wanted him to do, because it was what he wanted, too: He knelt and scraped a shallow hole at the roots and Frances, despite her bad knees, knelt with him. They buried the bottle with the winged figure until all that remained was a low dirt mound.

"Well done," Frances murmured, rubbing her palm up and down his arm, melting away all his shame in that single approving gesture. "Well done."

They stood. The mother cat glided out from beneath the back porch and watched from a safe distance with her flashbulb eyes, as if she'd also heard the story and was waiting for what came next. Then Dustin forgot his hunger and his thirst and his despair, he felt himself leaving his body and rising with his mother into that gentle sky where time slipped past unmeasured and both of them could still be changed.

YOUR ANGER IS A TINY BIRD

DUCK'S ON GUARD DUTY when the lights appear in the trees across the highway. He rouses Joyce, who gets Rina, who shakes awake Iris, who runs downstairs to the gift shop to wake me. It's hard to get me out of bed these days, even if that bed is a pile of beach towels and Virginia Tech sweatshirts heaped on the floor behind the defunct cash register. It's the iron deficiency, or depression. Probably both.

Still grumbling and stretching, I join the others on the welcome center's roof. It's a muggy August morning, about 5:00 a.m. judging from the sliver of moon suspended in the east. Duck's stripped off his oversized *I'd Rather Be in Richmond* T-shirt, baring his skinny brown chest. Iris and Rina test the points of our remaining arrows for sharpness. Joyce passes the binoculars to me so I can have a look: three shadowy figures bearing torches and marching down the pockmarked stretch of pavement that used to be the exit ramp. Unless they change course, they'll be on us in five minutes.

"Could be newcomers," says Iris. "Scavengers. Headed south for winter." She's twenty-two, wiry and blonde with small, alert eyes that rove and flick like green bugs. Once upon a time, she served as the wilderness guide back at the anger therapy retreat where most of us met. There's the unspoken understanding in our group that we'd all be dead without her knowledge of edible mushrooms and how to start a fire out of sticks.

"There's better pickings in the city," Rina says. "Scavengers would know that." She's notched an arrow to her bow. She looks quite formidable posed like that on the rooftop, the moonlight illuminating the taut lines of her arms, even if Iris is the only one of us who can shoot worth a damn. "I say we nab these suckers before they get us. They could be armed. We don't need any trouble."

I'm inclined to agree. We've only been settled in the welcome center a few months, but it's the best place we've found since we came down from the mountains last summer. The hunting's decent now that animals have started wandering into developed areas, and we're close enough to the city to make the occasional raid for food or medicine. Iris even has a little garden out back, just some tomatoes and carrots, but it's a treat to eat stuff that doesn't come from cans.

The breeze picks up. The Virginia state flag waves and snaps from its pole in the empty parking lot. I've been staring at the torches so long, my vision dances with orange spots. Still Rina doesn't move. For all her bravado, she, like the rest of us, is waiting for Joyce to speak.

Joyce takes the binoculars from me and studies the approaching figures again. In her early sixties, she's the oldest in our group by three decades, but it's not just age that gives her authority. Even back at the retreat, Joyce exuded a gruff sensibility that made it hard to believe she was just another hothead trying to keep her rage under control. I trusted her. Two years ago, when we stepped out of our cabins after the ten days of unplugged meditation, recovered our phones, and saw the news—the highways clogged with abandoned cars, whole cities shuddering into darkness—Joyce was the first to turn her back on the road and head higher into the mountains. Wait it out, she said. Nothing else we can do. Of the six who followed, Rina, Iris, and I remain. We picked up Duck last summer, the lone survivor in a suburb full of bodies, including his grandparents. He was Immune. For the first week he didn't say a word, not even his name, so Iris started calling him Duck, after the pond where we found him watching mallards chatter and dunk their heads underwater. He came around soon after, but said "Duck" was an improvement over his real name, which was too humiliating to say aloud.

"They're not making any secret of themselves, waving around that fire," says Joyce at last. She rests the binoculars on her thigh and turns to look at us. "It's possible that they're newcomers. Or maybe they know this place is occupied and they're looking to barter. We can't go around shooting people until we're sure. Rina and I will figure out what they want. Iris, Duck, and Sandy—stay here. Be ready if things go south."

With just the three of us up there, the darkness seems to thicken, settling on our bodies like a shroud. Duck scoots up against the chimney, breathing shallow. Iris grabs the bow and arrow Rina abandoned. A low chant slips from under her breath: "Your anger is a roof tile. Your anger is a piece of toast."

I lower myself until I'm lying on my stomach, shingles scraping my elbows. Nightmare after nightmare races through my head. I think about the wild men that sprang on us last winter and ripped out chunks of Rina's hair. I think about the gibbering Survivors we still sometimes pass on the road, tongues lolling, limbs stained with the sprawling pink rash of the virus that refused to kill them. I think about the people we've lost: Terrie, our retreat therapist, to a stomach infection. Cameron to some paranoid lunatic with a rifle. Molly to the virus itself. She'd started showing symptoms after she and Duck raided an elementary school cafeteria for canned goods last year. She wandered off to the highway to die alone.

The breeze continues to swell. I peek over the crest of the roof to see the strangers have stopped at the edge of our parking lot. Their torch flames gutter violently. Above the creaking tree branches, the snapping of the flag, I make out the distinct lilt of a human voice.

"What are they saying?" asks Iris.

The voice cries out again, high and ghostly. I shake my head.

"Something about right? Or *fight*? Are they challenging us to a fight?"

Duck peers out from behind the chimney. The early pink glow of dawn rims the eastern sky. In its faint blush I can see him pinch his chin in concentration. He's fourteen, and when I'm not completely aggravated with him for stomping around on his big flat boy feet when I'm trying to sleep, or forgetting to boil the drinking water, I feel bad. The rest of us got to finish adolescence. We got to graduate high school. Leave our parents' homes. Drive cars.

"I think," Duck says slowly, "I think they're saying, *We bring you the light.*"

It used to be we dreamed of rescue, the beating of helicopter blades in the night. NATO. The Red Cross. The UN. "The good guys," Molly used to call them interchangeably. Molly possessed the tired optimism and dead-eyed grin that are survival staples in the food service industry. We were both servers at Russell & Russell Catering Company. When I had my meltdown and started chucking fistfuls of cake around the dining hall, Molly joined in. It was a surprise to both of us. "I never realized how much I hate this job," she said thoughtfully as we sat on the loading dock licking frosting off our hands, counting down the seconds until we were both canned.

But the Russell sisters wanted to make a different example out of us and sent us to five weeks of anger management therapy instead.

We went quietly. The reality of our situations had reemerged with crystal clarity in the aftermath of our tantrums: Molly and I couldn't afford to lose our jobs. We signed up for the ten-day Allegheny retreat because it promised an accelerated path to the program's certificate of completion. Hospitals on the West Coast were already flooded with cases of a mystery airborne virus, but we didn't think much of it. Like the flu, it seemed to threaten mostly the very young and very old, with everyone in between pulling through.

Unbeknownst to us, the thing behaved more like a computer virus than a biological illness. It learned and mutated with incredible speed. It played tricks on doctors: It would appear to clear a patient's system only to resurface, more virulent than before, once the person was discharged onto packed buses and crowded streets. By the time the government and the WHO and whoever else got their act together, there were tens of thousands of cases in every state. The virus, as far as I know, never even got a name.

There's little optimism in our group since we lost Molly. The UN, if it exists anymore, won't be coming for us. We look out for each other. Strangers fill us with suspicion. After the torchbearers go back the way they came, leaving a single flame blazing in the parking lot, we wait until full daylight to investigate.

The fire's burned out. Pinned to the pavement under the chunk of brick that holds the torch upright, Joyce finds a note. What's remarkable is that it's not scrawled on the back of a page torn from a book, or a faded "Lost Cat" flyer stripped from a fence post. This paper is thick and beige with soft, frayed edges. Homemade. The ink is dark blue, the handwriting so lovely it appears stenciled.

"'To our sisters and brother at the welcome center,'" Joyce reads aloud. "'We have observed your fortitude from a respectful distance and believe you would make a fine addition to our family. We are the Mother Earthlings, a peaceful, God-fearing clan that hopes to repopulate our ravaged world, to learn from the mistakes of our forebears and create a new era where humanity lives in harmony with the natural environment.'"

"Oh God," says Rina with distaste. "Religious freaks."

"*Respectful distance?*" I repeat. "What does that mean?" I cast nervous glances around the parking lot, at the rusted red Chevy with its old birds' nests in the bed and the tall grasses waving along the exit ramp—grasses, I realize, where it would be easy for a person to lie still and watch our comings and goings.

Joyce flips over the paper and reads on: "'In a day's time, we will send an envoy to treat with you in person and, we sincerely hope, lead you back to our home where you will enjoy all the comforts of living in a well-secured community with good-hearted people. Stronger Together . . .' And then it's just signed, *Mother Earthlings*."

Duck's mouth falls open. Rina chews a greasy strand of her hair. We've had our dealings with individuals, even brushed paths with the occasional small band of Uninfected or Immune like ourselves. The concept of a whole society with a name and a philosophy is new to us.

"It's a trap," I say.

"You can't know that," says Iris.

"It's a *cult*." I grab the paper from Joyce and wave it in Iris's face. "Did you not hear any of this? *God-fearing clan, repopulate the Earth*. And they've been watching us. They knew we were four women and a boy." Something hot and jagged, like a boiling shard of glass, seems to be working its way through my brain: the hard edge of an anger I haven't felt in a long time.

"Religion is a source of hope for some people," says Iris calmly. "You don't have to judge them for it. And I'd watch a group of newcomers before I approached them, too. Fact is, it sounds like these folks have a permanent settlement. Isn't that what we've been after all along? Isn't that what we've been trying to make right here?"

It's unclear what we've been trying to make, other than a chain of days that might lead to months that might lead to some semblance of a life.

Joyce is quiet. Rina snatches the paper from me and rereads it, beady eyes slotting back and forth across the page. The boiling shard of glass has become a molten pool, spreading across my forehead. I turn and stalk past the Chevy toward the welcome center. I've never been good at pinpointing the cause of my anger—one of the reasons I probably wouldn't have earned that certificate even if the world hadn't ended—but I'm wallowing in it now, the driving spark, the heat familiar as sex.

I pace through the gift shop's aisles with their racks of T-shirts and shiny postcards. I seize a snow globe and shake it, watching the white confetti whirl crazily around a miniature downtown Richmond. It's enlivening, the way this fury overtakes my whole body, but it's also terrifying. More than once I have thought of it as a kind of virus.

I take a deep breath. "Your anger is a penny," I say in a low monotone. "Your anger is a snow globe. Your anger is bundles of sticks."

It began as a little game back at the retreat, something we did to mock Terrie, who was always coming up with dumb metaphors for our rage. *Imagine your anger is a marble: now slip it into your pocket. Imagine your anger is a tiny bird: now lock it in a cage.* In those first days after we emerged from our cabins and saw the state of things, as the hunger and terror and grief set in, the sayings became much more. They were a mantra, each word a good luck charm, a reminder of what we were still alive to feel.

"Your anger is a mouse," I murmur. "Your anger is a tree." Between gaps in the shelves pushed up against the windows, I see our ragtag little group still gathered in a circle around the burnt-out torch, and my head soars with a different feeling. A kind of love-rage, fierce and protective. Those three women and that teenage boy are all I have left in this world.

In the apocalypse, everybody looks like someone I used to know. The giggling Survivor we passed on our way into Maryland, pink rash blotting his naked back, could've been the middle school gym teacher who scrawled "needs improvement" on each one of my report cards. Another Survivor recalled the broad heavy features of my mother, whom I hadn't spoken to since I left home after high school. Bloated bodies took the shapes of roommates, classmates,

ex-girlfriends, neighbors, distant cousins, the cashiers at Giant
Eagle where I used to stop after work to grab something ready-
made for dinner. It was eerie, but like everything else, I got used
to it. I've learned to overlook the resemblances. To accept that my
mind is playing tricks.

This is why, when the Mother Earthling envoy swaggers into
our parking lot the following morning and I catch her face through
the binoculars, I don't immediately react. I don't say a word to
Duck or Rina on the rooftop beside me. My heart doesn't throb
with the jolt of recognition. At least, not until Duck takes his turn
with the binoculars and half-shouts, eyes still glued to the plastic
eyepieces, "Holy shit, isn't that Molly?"

I go flying through the trapdoor and descend the pull-down
staircase and a second set of stairs and sprint into the lobby where
Joyce grabs hold of me at the exit: "Sandy, no, no, she could still
be Infected. Don't—" I shove her off and burst through the glass
doors into the sunny parking lot. I run right up to Molly and
embrace her.

"Goddamn you," I say with my face buried in her shoulder.
"We all thought you were dead."

"So did I," says Molly.

We step apart. It really is her: same curly black hair, same
small ears and dimples and lopsided smile. In the fog of my relief,
the differences penetrate more slowly. She wears a kind of flowy
beige smock, not the filthy T-shirt and cargo shorts in which I saw
her last. Instead of the sneakers with the faded soles, her feet are
encased in sandals that look like little baskets, woven together from
strips of what might be leather. And her face—something different
there, too. The roundness of contentment, of regular meals. Her
whole body seems fuller, now that I'm looking, the smock unable
to conceal the slight hill of her belly that pressed against me when
we hugged.

Before I can say anything else, the doors to the welcome center
open and Duck trots into the parking lot. He allows Molly to hug

him, though the look on his face betrays an uneasy bemusement I'm also starting to feel. "I have so much to tell both of you," says Molly. "Come here, let's sit. There's some shade over there . . ."

As we follow her toward the black oak tree that stands at the edge of the lot, Duck leans toward me and whispers, "Molly's gotten kinda fat."

"She's not fat, you dingbat," I snap. "She's pregnant."

If Molly's pissed at not receiving a warmer welcome from her old gang, she doesn't show it. In the tree's dark pool of shade, she sits with her legs crossed, back resting against the trunk. She tells us how quickly the virus overtook her after she'd gotten exposed at the elementary school—the crippling fatigue, the fever that filled her with hallucinations of her forehead bursting open. On the median of I-64, she collapsed.

"And then they found me," she says.

"Who?" I ask.

"The Mother Earthlings. They took me in. Healed me. It was a miracle. But I was worried I'd never see you guys again. When I heard about the group at the welcome center, I thought there might be a chance. I begged to come see you. They didn't want me to overexert myself." She gestures at her stomach, and I feel a queasy lurch inside my own. "But the thing is, they can't really say no to me. They can't say no to any of the women. We're the future. We get the best food, the best sleeping spots. We hardly have to do any work around camp." Her eyes shine with satisfaction.

"So who's the dad?" blurts Duck. I want to smack him, but Molly waves a hand indifferently.

"Oh, just some kid at camp. I think his name's Marco?"

Behind us, Joyce has got her head and shoulders hanging out the welcome center door. Sunlight turns the windows black with glare, but I imagine Iris and Rina standing in the lobby, noses pressed to glass.

"They sent me out to see whether you were sick," says Duck. "I should go back. I'll tell them what you said."

Then it's just the two of us, as it had so often seemed to be at Russell & Russell Catering Co. Molly and I balancing big white plates on our forearms, navigating that sea of white faces. Molly and I cramming leftover bruschetta and pot stickers into our mouths before the busboys could toss them in the trash. Molly and I, drunk one night on a pilfered bottle of Pinot Grigio, tangled together on a vast glossy lawn in the dark, high-pitched laughter turning into something breathy and serious, fingers undoing with surprising deftness the buttons on each other's matching caterer's vests. I missed her more than I realized—she was the one holdover from that old life when making rent was my biggest concern—but I can't shake off my disquiet.

"How are you here?" I ask.

"I told you, the Mother Earthlings healed me."

"They had drugs? Antibiotics?"

"No drugs."

I stare at her incredulously. Molly raises her arms in surrender. "Look, I wouldn't have believed it was possible either, but here I am. I've got a life now. I've got a chance to contribute. And you could, too."

"What, by getting knocked up?" My fury is returning. I can't help it. *Your anger is a fetus. Your anger is a flowy smock.* "You spread your legs for a nice sleeping spot."

"Don't be so dramatic. I'm thinking about the big picture. Repopulation is our number one priority. And why shouldn't I be rewarded for doing that work? Lord knows it's not easy."

"I don't sleep with men," I say. "Last time I checked, neither do you."

"Oh Sandy," she sighs. "It's the end of the world. Does that stuff really matter anymore?"

Joyce, Iris, and Duck join us outside. They bring our cooking gear along with canned green beans, a box of expired linguine, and some tomatoes from Iris's garden—the fixings of a feast. Joyce builds a fire. Iris and Duck batter Molly with questions. How many Mother Earthlings live at the camp? Are there other Survivors? Does everyone have to wear those ugly smocks?

Molly's responses paint a picture of a hard-working community of roughly eighty individuals—Survivors, Uninfected, and even a few Immune like Duck, who watched family die around them but never experienced a symptom. Work is divided up. You have the hunters and the foragers, the cooks and the builders, the healers and the planters. With so many people working toward a common end, there's even time for things like games and singing.

"Sandy thinks you guys are a religious cult," says Iris.

"It's not like that. Some people are religious. But if there's any predominant belief, it's belief in Mother Earth. Respect for her."

"If the earth's our mother, she's doing a shit job at parenting," I say. "She's been trying to kill us for months. Between the cold and the heat and the poisonous plants . . ."

Joyce laughs. But the others aren't listening to me. I'm the crotchety grandma at the family reunion. The spit on the birthday cake. As Molly describes the Mother Earthlings' garden—a veritable Eden compared to Iris's paltry patch out back—I stand and cross the parking lot. It's past noon. The humidity covers me like plastic wrap. Before the end of the day, Molly will return to the Mother Earthling camp with our willing group members in tow. I can't imagine saying goodbye to her so soon after her resurrection, but I can't imagine following her, either.

I find Rina sulking on one of the red plastic benches in the McDonald's, her tangled brown hair tied back with a length of twine that came off a yoyo from the gift shop.

"She's not Infected," I say, sitting across from her. "You know that."

"If she doesn't have the virus now, then she never had it," says

Rina flatly. "I know a scam when I see one. Where's the rash?" She shakes her head. "Any of them actually thinking about going with her?"

"Iris. Maybe Duck."

"They're idiots."

"They're young. They want a chance at something more. Relationships. A family."

"And you?"

I spread my hands on the table and study my fingers, the stubby nails packed with dirt. In group therapy I could never bear to make eye contact with those women blabbing about their pasts. When it was my turn to speak, I usually just made something up.

"When I was sixteen," I say, "my parents sent me to this camp to try and rewire me. It was chock-full of people preaching about procreation, a woman's body as a vessel. Like I was totally empty unless I had a baby inside me. They said we were put on earth for one thing, and that was to be fruitful and multiply. I don't see how these Mother Earthlings are any different."

The McDonald's faces the creek that fronts the north side of the welcome center. Rina and I sit and stare out the windows for a bit, not speaking. Suddenly she laughs. "All these people talking about repopulation, the renewal of the human species, and no one asks the question of whether we deserve to survive. I mean, fuck. Mother Earth's doing great without us. No bulldozers. No weed whackers. No oil spills."

"Your anger is a weed whacker," I say. "Your anger is an oil spill."

The two of us go about the rest of our day like nothing has changed. We boil buckets of water at the camp stove we took from Home Depot last month. We check on the leftover venison that's submerged in the creek inside a bag inside a metal lunchbox to keep it cool. We water Iris's vegetable garden. We take inventory of our non-perishables. There's only enough canned chili, peanut butter, energy bars, tuna, and raisins to last us the next two weeks. This means more trips into basements and cafeterias. More risks of exposure.

The others stay outside all afternoon. They follow the shade as it moves clockwise around the base of the oak tree. The shadows are long, the sun slanting toward the horizon, when Duck and Iris return to the welcome center to collect their things. There's not much. A single backpack for each.

"You sure about this?" I ask Duck.

"No." His foot jiggles anxiously on the linoleum. "But, like, it could be cool, right? Maybe there'll be some dudes my age to hang out with. Not that I don't like hanging out with you guys," he adds quickly. "You guys are dope. And I'll come back and visit, right?"

"Right," I say. Even though the welcome center feels too big for three people. Even though I suspect we'll be packing up and moving farther south within the week.

Joyce prowls around the gift shop, maybe double-checking whether Duck and Iris grabbed all their things, maybe trying to avoid saying goodbye.

"What," I say, "you don't want to be a Mother Earthling?"

"This body's mothered all it's ever going to," says Joyce. She leans up against the counter with her sunburned arms folded against her chest. "I'm surprised to see you're not packing up to go live in peace and harmony with your girl."

"She's not *my girl*. She's gone off the deep end with this crap."

"I don't know. Maybe they have a point. If I were thirty years younger, who's to say I wouldn't want to contribute? You're, what, twenty-eight? Twenty-nine? You should be thinking about the long-term."

I shake my head in disgust. "You know, I thought you of all people would be on my side. Yeah, fine, the world is over. But that doesn't mean I have to let go of everything. My identity, and my self-worth . . ." I feel myself working up to a real good rage. Then I notice that Joyce is chuckling.

"Relax," she says. "I'm just pulling your leg. It's good to see you angry again."

"Terrie told us anger's not productive. It won't get us anyplace we want to go."

"Terrie, God rest her soul," says Joyce, "didn't know shit about anger. Anger's the only reason we're alive."

It's nearly sunset by the time everyone's done milling around saying their goodbyes. Iris and Duck light torches. In the parking lot, Molly gives me another hug.

"You know no one would force you to do anything you don't want to. I hope you'll reconsider, Sandy. I really do."

"Don't count on it," I say.

A hand clasping either one of my shoulders, she holds me at arm's length. "Why won't you trust me?" she asks softly.

"Why won't I trust you? Because you've been brainwashed! Those nutcases convinced you that they saved you from a sickness you never had, and now you think you owe them something. And what happens when you have the kid? You gonna have another one, and another one after that? What happens when you can't have any more?"

Molly's arms drop to her sides. I think for a moment that I've really hurt her, and I'm sorry. She glances back at the welcome center where torchlight scatters shadows across the sidewalk. Then, in a single swift movement, she pulls up the front of her smock, and in the glow of the setting sun I see the familiar rosy stains blossoming across her breasts and the swell of her stomach. They're almost beautiful. Like a child's rendition of springtime. I'm struck by the urge to reach out and touch it, this rash I've only ever seen from a safe distance. As the others step out the doors into the parking lot, Molly drops the smock to cover herself again.

"Goodbye, goodbye!" chants Duck, tap-dancing his way across the pavement. "Adios! Aloha! Fare thee well!" He's being goofy, I know, to conceal the strain of departure. Iris gives me a hug. We haven't always gotten along, but I realize that I'll miss her, too. She joins Duck and Molly: three people holding three sputtering torches, only this time they're headed away from me. They're crossing the parking lot, wading through the grasses toward the exit ramp and the empty highway and the trees waiting beyond.

So that's it, I think to myself dully. Our precious family of two years: fractured clean in half. I'm feeling exhausted again. How badly I'd like to curl up in my nest behind the cash register and sleep for decades. When I wake, nature will have won its slow war of reclamation. Tree roots will buckle and crack concrete. Woodland animals will occupy every ruined home, forging burrows from the detritus of all that gone life. Stubborn holdouts like the Mother Earthlings might have their square of land on which to plant fruit trees and weave their homemade sandals. But repopulate the earth? Give me a break.

Rina nudges me. "C'mon. Joyce wants a meeting."

Of course she does. No matter how many people we lose, there's still the looming unknown of tomorrow to prepare for.

I follow Rina around the back of the welcome center where Joyce has built another fire. Its meager light laps at her face and bounces off the round object she offers me in the palm of her hand: a snow globe. A shoebox filled with them rests at her feet. She must've gone through the gift shop, ransacking every shelf.

"What are we doing here, Joyce?"

"You know," she says shrewdly, and I realize that I do, for what enraged woman hasn't longed for a secret box of breakable things that will shatter with such majesty into a hundred shining fragments? I accept the snow globe, glancing briefly at the smiling cartoon cardinal suspended inside. Then I hurl it against the building. The sound is everything I hoped it would be, a resounding and triumphant answer to the helpless roar that's been building inside me for years. Rina and Joyce take their turns, and I go again, and for just those few minutes until the box runs empty, the night is alive with tiny glass explosions.

SNOW GIRL

MARCY GREER WAS BORN in summer, but winter followed her like a shadow, like a long, snowy cloak. The first time it happened: the metal flavor of frost in her mouth, the white burst of a snowball against her brother's head. He'd committed some crime or other—maybe touching her toys without permission—and the blizzard of Marcy's fury was biting and swift. By the time her parents caught on, David was so buried only the hairs at the top of his head protruded.

They lived in a valley in upstate New York. November through April, the place was a snow-filled trench and Marcy's "accidents" were camouflaged easily enough. The problem was summer. Rose Greer, who'd quit work to teach her daughter at home, tacked a calendar to the bulletin board next to the faded world map. For every ten days Marcy went without spitting snow, a treat awaited her at the breakfast table: gel pens, barrettes, erasers shaped like tropical fish. Jacob Greer made threats. "You screw up," he growled, "you answer to *me*," though he was the sort of huge, hulking man who'd never hit a person in his life, all bluster and lumber, and Marcy knew it even then.

The incident that exposed her would forever be remembered as the September freak storm of 2000. Marcy was ten, and the family dog, who liked to wander, had just come up dead under the wheels of Mr. Kistler's tractor. Marcy marched onto the neighbor's farm and planted herself in the aisle between trees, branches bowed with the shiny red plumpness of Jonagolds and Honeycrisps. She opened her mouth and screamed. Snow surged from her lips and eyes and nose, from the tips of her fingers and the ends of her hair, fat drifts crashing apple trees into splinters. CNN broadcast the story accompanied by clips of gleeful children building igloos in flip-flops. "A meteorological anomaly," the storm was formally dubbed. But Mrs. Kistler had seen, and soon the whole town knew bits of the story—not enough to fully believe it, just enough to give the Greer place a wide berth.

The details of that day remained fuzzy to Marcy. Sometimes, watching nature documentaries with David, witnessing an elephant stampede or a white shark breach, she felt like she could call up a similar power, mighty and mindless, an ancient force blowing beneath her skin. Most of the time, she was helpless. She stood in front of the mirror each morning plucking ice chips from her bleeding lips. The storms came upon her without warning: dinnertime blizzards blasting cutlery off the table, ice driving cracks into the floor. Water damage covered the ceiling in rusty rings. The house succumbed to a slow ruin, and Marcy's parents along with it. Rose chipped ice from the countertops with a butter knife, glassy-eyed and grinning. "Never mind—you'll outgrow it!" (To the contrary: It seemed to Marcy that she was growing *into* her snowing, the blizzards getting more severe with the onset of puberty). Jacob took on double shifts at the auto yard to try and cover the cost of repairs. He was rarely home, and when he was, he slept on the living room couch in a nest of old blankets, looking more and more like a stranger who'd wandered in and collapsed at the first available place.

Only David remained cheerful, her sole companion and comfort. He pointed to the family dramas they liked to watch on TV after dinner, absurd shows with cyborg stepfathers and long-lost, vindictive twins. "See?" he said. "We have it *much* better than them." When freezing mucus clogged Marcy's sinuses, he brought a hot wash rag to lay against her face.

The day after Marcy's thirteenth birthday, her parents sat her down and explained about the hospital. For years, Rose had driven her to visit baffled allergists and neurologists, but these people, she assured Marcy, they were the real deal. International experts. The best of the best. Already they'd assembled a small group of patients with similar conditions—bringers of strange weather who, like Marcy, had spent their lives searching for the elusive cure.

"You'll go, get fixed, come back," said Jacob with his usual gruffness, and Marcy wanted to ask if he really thought it would be that simple. But what choice did she have? Didn't she and her parents want the same thing? She looked around the living room with its water-warped floors. On the table sat plastic forks and paper plates from yesterday's birthday party, a housefly buzzing over the dollops of dried frosting. Marcy had no friends to invite, so it had just been the four of them, she feigning enthusiasm at each unwrapped doll and glittery notebook and other things she'd long ago outgrown.

The hospital was in the desert. Red rock stretched for miles around the cluster of unassuming buildings, reminding Marcy of a movie she and David had seen about a colony on Mars.

After she said goodbye to her parents, the hospital director, a thin man named Dr. Rhee, led Marcy to the dayroom where she could meet the others: Alma from Oakland, who caused small earthquakes when she sneezed. Eloise from Plano, whose fingers itched with secret lightning. Glynn from New Orleans, summoner of smoke and fog. Marcy tried to hide her disappointment. Her whole life, she'd dreamed of girls out there like her. She'd imagined them swooping through her bedroom window like eagles, bearing her off to a mountainside where they were all worshipped as queens. But these girls were just girls. Pimples speckled Alma's chin. Eloise wore neon sportswear and a sour expression. Glynn smiled, revealing braces gummed up with hospital cafeteria food.

"Dr. Rhee," she said plaintively, "the TV's doing that thingy again." And while the director bustled into the corner to mutter and thump a fist against the box set, Marcy found herself shrinking under the gazes of her fellow patients.

"What're you in for?" demanded Alma.

Marcy explained about the snowing.

"Ha!" cried Eloise. "That's five dollars for me."

"Your money was on flooding," said Glynn. "And you said it would be a boy."

"I hoped it would be a boy because I'm tired of you idiots. And a snowstorm can easily turn into a flood. *Duh.* Once it *melts.* Right, Marcy?"

"I guess," said Marcy, fiddling with the straps of her backpack.

"You *guess?*" Eloise unfolded her long legs and rose from the couch. She was no taller than Marcy, but her puffed-up halo of staticky blonde hair gave her an impression of great size. "You wanna know what I'm in for? I shot lightning bolts through the roof of my school. Classes were canceled for a week. There're still scorch marks on the wall." Leaning in toward Marcy, she whispered, "They say I'm *crazy.* I'm a force to be *reckoned* with." She lifted a finger and set it against the hollow of Marcy's throat. It was only the slightest shock, the kind Marcy had received a hundred times touching door handles in winter, but she leapt as if slapped.

There wasn't much to unpack. Some hair ties and clothes. The ratty stuffed pig her parents had bought her as a toddler. Her clock radio. A grape-flavored lip balm that, after careful consideration, Marcy placed on the chest at the foot of the bed. She had opted to leave her *Harry Potter* books at home for David—a decision she now regretted as she felt the smothering expanse of her boredom creeping in on her.

A window glared from her bedroom into the hall. Drawing back the paper blinds, Marcy could see straight into Alma's room across the way. Rock music thudded from an unseen boom box. Alma floated back and forth past the window, arms flickering, head bopping—a bizarre, graceful dance from which Marcy couldn't look away. She knew so little about girls her own age. Were they all so uninhibited when they thought no one was watching? Even when she was alone, Marcy treaded softly. She didn't sing in the shower. She didn't pout and preen before the mirror like the girls on sitcoms. She didn't lust after boys, real or imagined. Lately she'd begun to wonder if the snowing hadn't cursed her with a different, more far-reaching kind of coldness: a numbness toward things that should have made her happy.

Alma halted, her back to the window. She wore a too-large pajama tank top that slid off one shoulder. Her body tensed. Buckled. Marcy couldn't hear the sneeze, but the force of the tremor toppled her onto the floor. She looked up, dazed, as the bedroom lights flickered. From down the hall, Eloise's voice screamed, "Goddammit, Alma!" Marcy raised herself to the window. The rock music had cut out, and Alma's blinds were closed.

She wouldn't have thought it possible to adapt as quickly as she did to the hospital's routine. Morning lessons with her stammering tutor in the dayroom. A battery of medical tests in the afternoons: scopes probing, needles pricking, an endless rotation of geneticists, neurologists, and endocrinologists asking the same questions over and over. Could she describe the pre-snow sensation? Could she pinpoint circumstances where it seemed likely to happen? Could she remember when she first experienced the urge to snow at people? That last question annoyed Marcy more than the rest combined. She felt like asking the doctors if they remembered when they first felt the urge to *not* snow at people.

Evenings, Marcy called home to talk to David. The telephone outside the dayroom had a strange, cheesy smell. The hallway, with its high ceilings and walls sponged to look like clouds, gave an unsettling impression of infinity.

"And she's read *Order of the Phoenix* three times already," finished David triumphantly. He was talking about the new girl in his fourth-grade glass, Becky something. Together, they had joined the school chorus and the Newbery Club. Marcy wanted to be happy for him. Her brother had been so intent on keeping her company during her indoor seclusions that he hadn't made friends his own age. But the thought of David laughing and learning with a stranger raised an icy burn in Marcy's throat. She turned her head from the receiver and coughed slush into her palm.

"Dad?" she asked.

"Still on the couch." David lowered his voice. "Some nights he doesn't even come home. Mom says he gets back from the auto yard late and leaves before I get up, but I've been waking up in the middle of the night to check. Where d'you think he goes?"

"Maybe he has another family."

She meant it as a joke, but David, after a thoughtful pause, said, "Yeah, maybe. Should I follow him, d'you think? Check out the situation and report back?"

Marcy had a mental image of her brother creeping between used cars, stumbling on stray bumpers and broken glass. "No. Definitely not. Listen, David. We just have to—to wait for him to come around. Weather the storm." She sounded like her mother, who chanted the same cautious mantras when she came on the line each night. *Just do what the doctors say. Be patient. Don't make a fuss.* The telephone emitted two sharp blips. Marcy, suddenly frantic, cried, "David? Are you there? Can you hear me? David!"

"I think it's the other line." His voice sounded tiny. Marcy pictured a car stealing him into a tunnel, farther and farther away. "I'll talk to you tomorrow. I love you. Goodnight."

She was prescribed a medicine that left a strong aftertaste of Cheerios. She was prescribed a medicine that made her wake in the night, streaked in cold sweat; that made her feet break out in itchy welts; that made her hair so hard and brittle, she could snap it like straw. She was prescribed a medicine administered as a shot into her abdomen three times a day. She was prescribed a medicine that she was no longer taking, stashing the pill under her tongue and flushing it down the toilet at the first chance, because the only commonality between all the medicines was their shared uselessness. Marcy's snowing remained worse than ever. Her teeth ached from the constant chill. Frostbite stained her toes and the tips of her ears, first white, then crimson. A nurse brought in wool socks and a furry hat. Marcy felt ridiculous shuffling into group therapy on Friday with her fuzzy ear flaps pulled low.

"It's a conspiracy," Glynn whispered. Her glasses fogged up when she got excited, transforming her into a misty-eyed bug. "They don't want us to get better. They want to harness our powers and use them on Al Qaeda. Rhee's just a figurehead. The board of directors is nothing but a bunch of government puppets . . ."

"You read too many comic books," said Eloise, who was cleaning under her fingernails with the corner of a *Seventeen* magazine.

"Who do you think is funding the hospital? Are your parents paying for you to be here? Are yours?" Glynn turned to Alma, who shrugged. "I mean, it's not even a real hospital. There are no other patients. The place looks like it was built in ten minutes."

She had a point there. They'd done what they could to make the facility look homey, but there was no hiding the leaky sinks, ill-fitting doors, or the paint blisters that Marcy scraped off her bedroom wall with a fingernail as she struggled to fall asleep.

Dr. Kline, a bony woman who wore too much jewelry, entered the room. Alma launched into speech before the psychiatrist sat down. "I've been thinking more about emotional triggers, ya know? Like how my older brothers used to push me around, and maybe that contributed to a sense of *powerlessness* . . ."

"Teacher's pet," muttered Eloise. She rubbed a blue spark between her middle finger and thumb. Marcy was hypnotized, watching that little ember bounce from fingertip to fingertip until it landed in Eloise's palm and she, with a bored expression, closed her hand to snuff it out.

Later that evening Marcy visited Eloise in her room. She felt intimidated as the door swung open. With her freckled nose and sun-bleached hair, the older girl looked as though she'd never experienced a cold day in her life.

"I want to learn to control it. Like you do," said Marcy. "How is it that you do that?"

"You gonna snitch on me?" demanded Eloise.

"No."

Eloise considered her. She was chewing several pieces of gum and made loud smacking noises as she maneuvered the clump from one side of her mouth to the other. Static rolled off her Cowboys T-shirt. Marcy felt it brushing her torso like a force-field. "I can't tell you how it is for you," said Eloise. "But for me it's a mental thing. Like there's a little box inside me where I keep all the things that drive me crazy, all the shit that makes me want to explode."

"Is the box hard to open?"

Eloise laughed. She snapped her fingers and a tangle of blue light sprang from them like fireworks.

"The hard part," she said, "is closing it."

Marcy began to focus on her snowing intermittently, whenever she could. It was strange, trying to channel something she'd worked so long to suppress. But having a task made it all more bearable:

the medical tests and the phone calls home and the algebra sessions with the tutor who was clearly afraid of Marcy, who jumped when she sniffed too loudly and speed-walked from the dayroom when the study session was complete.

The best was Quiet Time, imposed on the girls daily between 3:00 and 5:00 p.m. under the theory that silence and meditation were essential in soothing their afflictions. Cross-legged on her bedspread, Marcy closed her eyes and tried to track the chill coursing through her throat. Somehow she understood the anger that had proven productive for Eloise would get her nowhere. The snow lived in the bittersweet place between sadness and joy. Marcy thought about her parents. The sunburn that capped her father's bald head when he forgot to wear his hat to work. Her mother's strong, thin fingers wrapped around the butter knife. She thought about how David used to follow her around the house as a toddler, giggling, two sticky fingers hooked into the belt loop of her jeans. Then a mouthful of cold steam, a chill behind each eyeball, and Marcy felt snow spray from her lips and float to the floor. Her eyes watered. She laughed, and more snow tumbled out. She covered her mouth with her hands. Tried it again. Two, three, four times, until a cold puddle covered the floor and her lips were numb and freezing.

Across the hall, Alma had abandoned her Game Boy and was watching her closely. When Marcy got up to use the bathroom, she followed.

"You've gotta be careful," said Alma.

"I know what I'm doing." Marcy's voice reverberated against the bathroom's pink tile. For the first time in a long time, she felt strong. Capable. "I'm finally taking control. I'm learning how to do this thing on my terms."

"We don't get to make the terms."

"So I should be a kiss-ass like you? Tell them exactly what they want to hear?"

"Yeah," said Alma. She crossed the room and sat on the windowsill. The sun was a dazzling smudge through dappled glass, brightening her from behind. Her hair had thinned as well—Marcy could see shiny patches of scalp like just-healing scabs—and it was clear she'd lost weight, the rail of her collarbone protruding sharply.

"All that stuff with Dr. Kline," said Marcy. "You're just making it up?"

"These people don't want answers. They want to be proven right. And the sooner you tell them what they want to hear, the sooner you can get back home."

"What if you don't want to go back?" Marcy was surprised to hear herself. She certainly didn't want to stay at the hospital forever. Yet returning to New York was not the satisfying prospect it had once been. David was growing up. He wouldn't always be around to stave off her solitude. As for her mother and father, what did they know of Marcy other than her snowing? She thought of that last sad birthday party, the silly dolls beaming in their boxes, and felt her parents' longing to hold her in a state of early girlhood before she'd driven winter into their lives.

Alma had no answer, except to rise from the windowsill and give Marcy's hand a squeeze.

Dr. Rhee strongly recommended against the girls leaving the facility over the holidays. Too risky. The scope of their abilities remained unknown, in spite of the researchers' best efforts to quantify them. That was the latest focus: measurements. Exactly what temperature were Eloise's lightning fingers capable of reaching? Exactly how much light could infiltrate Glynn's fog? Exactly how much snow could Marcy deploy in one sitting? Six inches? Two feet? Paper gown stuck to her thighs with sweat, she'd bent and spat a flurry of snowflakes into a bucket while a doctor with a hanging belly— Marcy had long ago lost track of their names and who specialized in what—emitted chaste exclamations: "Whoa! My gosh! Would you look at that!" She returned to her room dazed, mouth so dry it was like she had scraped her tongue on asphalt.

Against medical advice, Glynn's parents appeared in the lobby the second week of December, a tall man and a short woman carrying an enormous sequin purse. They sat stiffly on a plastic bench while Dr. Rhee fluttered around them like a hummingbird and Glynn went to pack her things. "It's really not safe, Mr. and Mrs. Sanders. I know you've driven all this way, but we're still not sure what the patients are capable of and were an accident to happen . . ."

Mr. Sanders stood to his full height, dwarfing the doctor.

"Fight-fight-fight," breathed Eloise from where she, Marcy, and Alma had gathered on the first-floor landing to watch. Marcy, too, found herself craving a confrontation, an explosion to rattle the hospital's expensive machinery and the doctors' confidence that what they were doing was the right thing, the only thing. But before Mr. Sanders could open his mouth, his wife wedged her way in front of him, holding the big purse like a battering ram.

"It's clear that your expertise in these matters surpasses anything my husband and I could ever hope for, Dr. Rhee," said Mrs. Sanders. "It's also clear that we're taking our daughter home for Christmas whether you want us to or not. We can stand here arguing all day, but these facts will never change."

The doctor had his back to the staircase so Marcy couldn't see his expression, but his voice was uncharacteristically cold as he handed a sheaf of papers to Glynn's mother. "The hospital is not liable for any damages the patient may cause while removed from our care. Sign and date."

It had all the makings of the most depressing holiday ever, yet Marcy couldn't remember a time when she'd had more fun. An orderly brought in a box of leftover decorations. Eloise flung glitter and ribbons through the dayroom, shrieking dirty versions of Christmas carols that carried all the way to the cafeteria where one of the night nurses had agreed to unlock the doors to the kitchen. Marcy ran her fingers over the gleaming chrome appliances while Alma sorted through the pantry's collection of non-perishables. "Green beans," she muttered to herself. "Cream of chicken, breadcrumbs . . . This could work." The nurse sat just outside in the cafeteria, painting her fingernails and humming along to Eloise's vulgar tunes.

"What are we making?" Marcy asked.

Alma handed her a can opener. "We're improvising."

"My mom could do that. You could hand her three ingredients and she'd figure something out. She always wanted a show on the Food Network. Like the Barefoot Contessa."

Alma laughed. "Like who?"

"The Barefoot Contessa! You know, she does recipes, and shows you, like, what flowers to buy . . ." She upended the cans over the casserole dish and combined the wet mess with a spatula. "Anyway, my mom's kitchen is a wreck now. I made a blizzard in there last spring and the insurance wouldn't cover the repairs, said it wasn't an *act of God*."

Alma slid the dish into the preheated oven. After a pause, she said, "They're afraid of me. My family. That's why they wouldn't come get me. Last Christmas, I destroyed my Tía Carla's apartment. Glass everywhere. Bookshelves on the floor. It was a nightmare."

Marcy leaned in and brushed her lips against Alma's cheek. She couldn't say what made her do it. Alma looked at her quizzically, but didn't pull away.

"I thought—" she said.

"What?"

"I thought you'd be cold."

Marcy raised two fingers to her own lips, suddenly self-conscious, but the skin there felt warm to the touch.

On Christmas morning, Marcy called home. The phone rang and rang. The cord cut a white coil into her skin as she wound it around her wrists. Finally a hoarse voice answered. Her father. Marcy was momentarily stunned. She hadn't spoken to him since leaving home almost four months ago.

"Hello?" he said irritably. "Hello? Dammit, it's Christmas. I don't want to buy any of your crap."

"Dad. It's me."

She heard what she thought might be the crackling of a fire. She imagined her father prodding the flaming logs with the poker, as he often did when nervous. "Your mother's gone to drop off some cookies with the Kistlers."

"Where's David?"

"Out with his snowboard. I finally caved and bought him one."

"Where have you *been*?" demanded Marcy.

Her dad chuckled. "I've been right here. You're the one who left home."

"David says you haven't been sleeping at the house."

"Your brother's just a kid. He doesn't know anything."

"So you bought him a snowboard and that's it, huh? Everything's okay. No hard feelings." She hadn't expected to be so angry. She hadn't even thought much about her father these past few months. But hearing his voice now, picturing him tucking into her mother's Christmas dinner like nothing had happened, and then leaving again, bringing his full belly to wherever it was he went . . . .

"You're the one who left home," he repeated sullenly.

"I was sent away," snapped Marcy. "You have a choice."

"I'm not about to be lectured by a teenager."

"So hang up."

She waited. Her father's breathing rasped over the line. Marcy had the phone cord wrapped so tightly around her hands, her fingers started to go numb. She slammed the plastic receiver into its cradle then retreated into the dayroom and sank onto the sofa. The arms were covered in dime-sized burns from where Eloise had drilled her fingers into the upholstery. It was so quiet. Alma and Eloise were still in bed. The dayroom's large rectangular window overlooked a rocky courtyard studded with small trees.

It didn't feel like Christmas without snow.

Marcy closed her eyes. Inhaled and exhaled, deep and steady, until a powdery carpet formed at her feet. She scooped up a handful of the snow. The soft cold weight felt familiar in her palm. She held it there, admiring its shine in the fluorescent light. She realized she no longer thought of it as a sickness. Her frostbitten ears had finally healed.

There was a new doctor at the hospital, a woman whose English rolled with a slight accent Marcy couldn't place. Dr. Ellstrom brought the four of them into Dr. Rhee's commandeered office the day after New Year's. Marcy had never been inside. She thought the place carried some of Rhee's nervous energy. Too many frames hung crookedly from the walls. The desk was covered in ornate puzzle boxes, which Dr. Ellstrom swept to one side as she sat in Rhee's chair. She kept touching her cropped hair at the ears and neckline, as if trying to accustom herself to a new style, while explaining her research team had uncovered a potential cure for the girls' illnesses. A permanent one.

"A simple procedure," she said, flashing a packet of consent forms. "These documents have been faxed to your parents for review."

"So we don't even get a say?" demanded Eloise. "It's our bodies."

Dr. Ellstrom turned her oddly colorless eyes onto Eloise. "Are you eighteen, Miss McCole?"

"No."

"Until such time as you come of age, your medical decisions will be made by your parents or legal guardians. And yours were the first to respond." Dr. Ellstrom held up another packet emblazoned with messy signatures, a little smugly, Marcy thought.

It came together quickly after that. Marcy heard Eloise scream-
ing protests into the phone outside the dayroom. "Her parents
are doctors," Alma said quietly. "Pathologists or something. They
trust the science." Eloise went to bed without saying goodnight.
For several minutes, Marcy stood outside her closed door and
thought about knocking, but to say what? I'm sorry? Congratula-
tions? Good luck? A cure was what they'd come here in search of.
Yet the thought of an Eloise without sparks at her fingertips filled
Marcy with sickening dread, like an Eloise without arms or eyes.

She went down the hall to Alma's room instead. Rock music
wailed from the boom box, but the floors didn't tremble. Alma,
too, had gained some sort of control over her sickness.

"I've been practicing," she said. "Like you. Watch." She sat
on the bed and closed her eyes. Her chest tightened with held
breath. Her mouth formed a small, tense line. A droplet of sweat
appeared on her temple and trailed down the side of her head.

"Alma," said Marcy. "You don't have to—"

"Just *wait*."

A guitar keened behind angry lyrics she couldn't make out.
Then the song ended, and in the seconds-long pause between one
track and the next, she felt it: an invisible force jolting the legs of
the bed, a haphazard pounding like an arrhythmic heartbeat.

They wouldn't get a chance to speak to Eloise again. After the
surgery, she packed her belongings while Marcy, Alma, and
Glynn were with their tutors. Marcy only happened to glimpse
the older girl as she was being escorted into the parking lot by a
harassed-looking redhead who could only be her mother.

"Eloise," Marcy called.

Eloise stiffened as if expecting a blow, or trying to absorb one
without making a sound. She speed-walked out of the building,

the wheels of her suitcase clacking over the tile. The red-haired woman granted Marcy a frowning once-over before following her daughter through the automatic doors.

Marcy called home that evening. Relief made her mother's voice ragged. Dr. Rhee had notified them about Eloise's successful surgery. As soon as Marcy had the procedure, she could come home. She could have her life back—or, rather, she could start the life she'd never been able to have. School. Friends. Plans for the future. David came on the line, talking about the sightseeing they would do together on the drive back to New York. Marcy had never been on a vacation. It had been too risky—snowstorms sweeping tourists into the Grand Canyon, wrecking rides at Disney.

"Hershey, Pennsylvania, Marcy!" proclaimed David. "The Sweetest Place on Earth! Did you know they have thirteen roller coasters? And chocolate bars the size of your whole body?"

At the first break in her brother's thrilled chatter, Marcy said, quietly but without hesitation, "I don't want to do this."

"Don't want to do what?"

"The surgery."

"You mean you don't want to get better? You don't want to come back and live with us?" He sounded quizzical. Marcy heard the rumble of a voice in the background. "Dad wants to talk to you," said David.

"What's this horseshit?" said Jacob. He kept his tone brisk, like he might just be teasing, but Marcy sensed the anger burning beneath his words. "You want to live at the hospital forever now, eh?"

"This cure isn't right," said Marcy.

"It worked for that other girl. The doctor told us all about it. A few tweaks in the brain, now she can lead a normal life. Don't you want that?"

"I—"

"This hasn't been easy for us, you know. Since you were just a little girl we've fought with the schools, we've taken you to specialists. People look at us funny in town."

"You never did anything. That was all Mom." She felt bad the moment she said it, because it wasn't true. Her father had taken those extra shifts at the auto yard. Uncomplainingly, he'd repaired or replaced the furniture her blizzards had destroyed. And it was he who'd convinced Rose to let Marcy enjoy the occasional excursion outside the house, to the movie theater or the mall. That was before the couch-sleeping and the long stints away from home. Did what came later negate what had come before?

The line was silent for a long while, but Marcy heard the crackle of static and knew her father hadn't hung up.

"All right. Maybe I wasn't what I could've been," he said. "But Jesus, Marcy—God knows I never signed on for—and your mother was hardly—" His voice quavered. Marcy found herself wishing he would've yelled at her instead. She placed a hand flat against one of the painted clouds on the wall and imagined shoving it so hard, it peeled away and streaked toward the sky.

Jacob cleared his throat. "We'll drive down to pick you up on Tuesday. All of us. Your brother can't wait to see you. And you won't disappoint him, Marcy."

The dayroom felt more stagnant than usual that evening. Marcy shuffled the same deck of sticky cards over and over. Glynn came down to use the phone, then Alma. No nurses appeared to tell them it was past curfew. The whole hospital had been swallowed inside a terrible calm. Ten o'clock found the three of them still sitting there while an orderly pushed a mop down the hallway, the squeak of his shoes grating like a chainsaw in Marcy's ears. She tried to corral her feelings, to summon some semblance of gratitude or joy that she'd soon be returning to her family, forever freed from the bite of ice in her throat. All she felt was disappointment. She realized a part of her had always hoped Glynn's conspiracy theory was true. She had wanted to believe they were important.

"Did you ever think you could use it?" asked Glynn. "Like a superhero?"

It was the first thing any of them had said in a half hour. Alma caught Marcy's eye as if to say, *there she goes again*, but Marcy replied right away: "Droughts. I could help people who don't have water. What about you?"

"There are always people who need hiding," said Glynn, her large, dark eyes shining mischievously behind their thick lenses. "People who need cover. Fog can be good for that."

They turned to Alma, who was piling checkers into a small tower on the table. "Construction work?" she said flatly. "Demolitions?"

"If you can make earthquakes," said Glynn, "maybe you can stop them. Just reach down low and turn them off. Think of all the people you could save."

"There *is* no saving," snapped Alma. "Don't you get it? This isn't one of your dumb comic books." A tremor rolled through the floor, shaking the furniture. The tower of checkers collapsed. "We're not superheroes. We're girls. Sick ones. Twenty years from now, this will all feel like some stupid summer camp, and I won't even remember your names."

They turned in around eleven. Marcy got into bed with Alma's harsh words still reverberating inside her head. She tried to mentally catalogue all the items in her bedroom back home—a trick she used to help her fall asleep in the past—but tonight the details were elusive. Did she keep the box of tissues on her nightstand, or her bookshelf? In which corner was the pale pink stain where David had once spilled a cup of fruit punch?

She didn't realize she'd fallen asleep until the fire alarm woke her. For one frightening moment, she had no idea where she was. Then her eyes found the familiar anchor of her clock radio: 12:07 a.m. She lurched into the hallway where the fog was already gathering, spreading and rising in a milky cloud. Alma appeared in the doorway to her room. Marcy barely had time to register her startled expression before the fog swung between them like a door.

They held hands, keeping to the walls while the smoke detectors shrieked and an automated message played on the hospital's PA system: *An emergency situation has been reported. Please stay calm and make your way to the nearest exit. An emergency situation has been reported . . . .*

The hospital's night staff shouted and blundered around them. A flashlight beam wavered like the lamp of a distant ship. Marcy shut her eyes and focused on remembering the route to the fire escape in the stairwell.

The fog dissipated once they pushed through the exit. The heavy door shut behind them, muffling the noises inside. The temperature had fallen with darkness, but the fire escape's metal railings still held the faint warmth of the sun.

Alma's bangs were a slick rectangle against her forehead. "What the hell was that?"

"Glynn," said Marcy. "Do you think she's running?"

"There's nowhere to go. She's just being stupid, trying to prove me wrong."

And yet they continued to stand there, watching the door, united in the slim possibility. Stars brightened the sky, more stars than Marcy had ever seen. The silence was sudden and expansive. Someone had finally turned off the alarm.

"I guess we should go back," said Alma.

"Yeah." Marcy reached for the fire door, but Alma's hand stopped her.

"I mean, there's no rush. We're already outside."

So they climbed up to the roof and looked at the stars. The night air sliced through Marcy's damp pajama shirt. She'd never known a desert could get so cold. Alma said it had something to do with lack of moisture: the heat, uncontained, whooshing up into space. Shivering, they dozed, curled around each other. Shadowy figures marched in and out of Marcy's dreams. They were like the girls she'd imagined as a child, but older and more terrible, with voices of thunder and mouths full of flame. Had Glynn gone to find them? Were they coming at last?

Then the winds of sleep scattered these images like so many grains of sand, and a new scene emerged, a different kind of sky, sunlight and fast-moving clouds, she and Alma flying down a desert road in a swiped car toward that line of mountains in the distance.

It was a dumb idea. Even dreaming, she knew it. Yet when the door to the stairwell clanged open below them, Marcy understood the teary burn in the back of her throat was neither relief nor terror, but the taste of a coming storm.

HAUNTING GROUNDS

EIGHT DAYS DEAD, NANCY Hayashi still hadn't found a decent place to haunt. This wasn't for lack of trying. Though in life she'd been a lazy woman—prone to whole days spent on the sofa, guilting her sons into delivering quesadillas and orange soda from the taco truck down the road—the afterlife had instilled in her a vitality she'd never known during eighty-two years of drawing breath. Nancy felt young again. The arthritic knots in her hands and shoulders had loosened. Her legs remained blue and swollen with fluid, but they didn't pain her like they used to. And in her chest: a sensation like double doors bursting open, admitting air and light and music into the shuttered room she'd become during those final, wretched days.

The problem was space. There simply wasn't enough. Nancy had long been of the opinion that there were too many people on earth. She saw now that the living had nothing on the dead. They hovered on rooftops and bridges, a spectral haze. They cluttered the bars behind restaurants and lounged in children's tree houses among the sleeping bags and smuggled snacks. They drifted in elevator shafts, unfazed as the big metal box sliced through their shimmering forms. They came from all eras and walks of life. During her first few days wandering, Nancy saw a girl with a scarlet Mohawk wedged in a defunct payphone booth with a plague doctor. On the same block, she encountered a small army of women in hoop skirts who had gathered on an apartment balcony to trade insults with the bikini-clad girl ghosts on the roof. Resentment was understandable. These people had spent their whole lives crammed among their fellows, forced to weigh their personal desires against the needs of an ever-expanding population. Now all they wanted was solitude and rest. Instead they were cursed with even more people, more anxieties about what belonged to whom and whether there would ever be enough.

Nancy soon gave up on the prime real estate, the cemeteries and churches that had been staked out long ago. Who needed those clichés anyway? She went to her old high school in Seattle, where she met her husband, where she was happy. The campus had long ago been bulldozed and a parking garage erected in its place. Ghosts were horizontally stacked on top of all the cars, as if reclining in invisible bunk beds. The light had a muted, undersea quality as it fell through their bodies. Only the twitch of a sneaker or occasional drawn-out sigh served to distinguish individuals from the towers of flesh.

So Nancy went to the hospital where she'd died, where she'd been miserable. But of course, many thousands of others had also died there and returned to swarm the bleak white halls. Even the gift shop was taken. A horde of ghost teenagers in flapping blue gowns chased her away from the racks of teddy bears and get-well-soon cards, shaking their translucent fists.

By the eighth day, Nancy's can-do perseverance started to ebb. She'd seen what happened to the ghosts that didn't find their haunting grounds in time. The lights in their eyes grew eerie and distant as candles behind fogged glass. They were blown about like scraps of newspaper in a damp breeze, directionless and forlorn. She held out hope for the little townhome where she and Lewis had raised the boys. She'd lived there her entire adult life and was sure she would've noticed if the place had been overrun by spirits. But her optimism withered before she'd even passed through the front

door: Three ghosts lolled in the garden beds among her hydran-
geas, and two more perched on the stoop. Inside, they were everywhere. On countertops, in closets, bobbing on the ceiling, and
sprawled across the floor. A ghost toddler had made a little throne
for himself on top of her grandmother's bronze lacquered vase.

"We're at maximum capacity," a ghost girl in overalls informed
Nancy.

"Can't you make an exception? I used to live here. My sons—"
She gestured at the dim outlines of her boys plodding around the
house, boxing up items for donation or sale. But the ghost girl
couldn't see them. Already Nancy's awareness of the living, so
strong on her first day risen, was fading, replaced with a newfound
capacity to perceive her fellow ghosts in minute detail. She could
count the pimples on the ghost girl's nose and see the white dust
clinging to her eyelashes.

"Have you tried the sewers?" suggested the ghost girl. "I heard
they've still got some space down there."

"Young lady," said Nancy. "I did not live for eighty-two years
so I could spend eternity watching people's crap pass me by. I may
be dead, but I have my dignity."

She felt her edges peeling away. The exposed soul smarted like a
fresh wound. She drifted, the toes of her slippers brushing grass.
She wondered why she hadn't met anyone she knew. Where was
Lewis? Where were her parents? Where was her little sister, Peggy,
who'd been born and died in Minidoka in 1943? Nancy forgot
their faces. The sun rose and set. Green hills rolled to the horizon.
Every so often, she looked up and found herself in a small town,
ghosts watching silently from windows and rooftops. They didn't
invite her inside. If they had, would she have gone? An old stub-
bornness swelled inside her, even as she faded. It simply would not
do to settle for any old place. She put her head down and kept
drifting. She began to chant to avoid losing herself entirely.

"I am Nancy Hayashi. I was born in Wapato, Washington in 1935."

"I am Nancy Hayashi. I was married to Lewis Hayashi, and our sons are named Lonnie and Mark."

"I am Nancy Hayashi. I was born in Wapato, Washington in 1935 . . ."

Her whole being shivered and thinned. She thought of an egg cracked and spreading across a scalding pan. She hardly heard herself. And yet the words must have acted as a compass: When she next looked up, Nancy faced a rundown farmhouse with a rusting roof and a kicked-in door—the place where she was born, and where her father tried to resettle the family after their release from Minidoka. The place where they tried to restart their helplessly stalled lives.

Nancy couldn't believe the house was still standing. It had been converted into some kind of garage. Filth encrusted the windows, but a single shaft of sunlight fell through a hole in the roof, illuminating the metal hulks of a dozen stripped cars. She drifted through the space where the door ought to have been and settled onto a dented hood. Someone had sliced through the vinyl top to access the interior. Glass sparkled all around her. Pigeons cooed from the rafters. Nancy smiled, blissfully adrift in a sudden, stretching calm. That was when the ghost descended from the ceiling with a pile of garbage in his arms.

"Hey. Who the hell are you? You can't stay here." It was the ghost of a middle-aged white man in a baseball cap and checkered shirt. His left leg was bloodstained and mangled. Bruises darkened his face. He threw the garbage aside. Soiled papers, crushed bottles, food wrappers, and balled-up plastic bags rained onto the hood of the nearest car.

"How are you doing that?" asked Nancy, impressed. "Every time I try to touch something, my fingers go right through it."

"Never mind *how am I doing that*. This spot's taken. I been here for thirty-five years and plan to stay here for the remainder of my afterlife. Alone."

"It's just you in here?"

"That's right." The ghost hovered a few feet above Nancy's head, his ruined leg floating at an odd angle. He gestured around the room. "You see these cars here? All mine. My brother and I found 'em, brought 'em here, took out their parts and pieced 'em together for new ones."

Nancy glanced at the skeletal machines, their gaping innards. "They look stolen."

The ghost man scowled. He floated higher, hands folded across his chest. "I'll have you know I was a law-abiding man all my life. Me and my brother both. Which is more than I can say for your type."

"My type?" said Nancy. He didn't elaborate, but she didn't need him to. She and her parents had only stayed in the farm-house a few months into that first winter of 1945 before a farmer came around to toss them out. He was a thin, balding man with fast-blinking eyes and hands that twisted the edges of his cap as he explained that the property belonged to him now, and would be rented to Mexican laborers in the spring. He didn't seem to relish the prospect of tossing the family into the cold, yet he did not bend, not even when Nancy's father, a man whose scrupulous pride had sustained them all through internment, dropped onto his knees and begged.

The ghost sorted the garbage into piles inside the gutted cars. He couldn't seem to leave it alone. "You still here?" he hollered.

She saw again the tremendous stillness in her mother's face as she folded their clothes into the suitcase, saw her father creasing the dollar bills he would slip inside each wool sock. Tenacity ran through her, then a hot spike like joy. *I am Nancy Hayashi, and I was born in Wapato, Washington in 1935.* "Yeah, I'm still here," she said. "And you know what? I kind of like the place." She ascended to the ceiling and spun in a slow circle, appraising the rafters gluey with pigeon shit. The ghost watched sulkily from below, a grimy liter bottle clenched in either fist. "Yes," said Nancy firmly. "I believe I'll make this place my home."

The longer she stayed in the farmhouse, the easier it became to pick things up. Her fingers caught on cobwebs and found purchase in the rotting walls, which she enjoyed clinging to like a spider before flinging herself gleefully into space. In no particular order, the textures of her old life returned. She remembered the citrus zing of orange soda; the calluses in the middle of Lewis's thumbs; the stripe of static in the hospital TV; that childhood funk her boys had carried in their clothes and hair when they returned from elementary school—dried sweat and French fries. She remembered, too, how on the day Peggy had died, a friend of her mother's from the camp—a woman she recalled now only as Auntie, though she had been no family relation—brought Nancy to the salon and pinned her hair into rolls the way she had always wanted.

Every afternoon, the ghost went out in search of more trash. Nancy didn't understand his fixation on the litter that blew through the overgrown field. She decided it must be an indicator of the garbage person he'd been while living. In this way, she began to suspect a kind of organizing justice in the afterlife. She'd always entertained a mild belief in God. She just didn't believe *he* had any interest in *her*. She and Lewis had that in common. A film lover, her husband had declared that if the life of the universe were a movie, he would be a funny sidekick at best and at worst, an extra passing on a crowded walkway—just an additional body meant to authenticate the experiences of the real stars. Nancy hoped that if Lewis had made it to this afterlife, he now felt singled out, special, *lucky*, the way Nancy did as she looped and soared in her weightless body.

She made a game of concealing herself in the rafters during the ghost's daily departures. Only after he'd floated back through the wall and performed a quick scan of the place did she zoom out of her hiding spot with a cry of, "Surprise!"

The ghost dropped his garbage and flapped his arms. He said things like: "Go on! Get out of here! Get out!" as if she were a squirrel that had slipped into the attic.

Then, switching tactics, he floated up beside her, adopted a goopy expression vaguely redolent of compassion, and said, "I know it can be hard to find our place. But there's a nice home waiting out there for you. Just keep looking, and you'll find it."

"Oh I've found my place," said Nancy. "Maybe it's you who should keep looking." She turned a half-dozen aerial backflips, and by the time she stuck the perfect landing, he was hurling obscenities at her again.

For the most part, though, they kept to their separate quadrants. The ghost ignored Nancy. He fussed with his garbage and slept— or what passed for sleeping in the afterlife: a deep state of dreamless relaxation—inside one of the cars. Sometimes he muttered to himself and gestured angrily. Stray words reached Nancy where she floated on her back near the rafters.

"Not now, Frederick."

"If I say the carburetor needs replacing, then that's what we'll goddamn do!"

Although Frederick was probably a friend or a son or the brother he'd mentioned, Nancy quickly attached the name to the ghost himself. *There goes Frederick*, she thought when he disappeared on his afternoon searches. And with the name came a host of questions that Nancy pondered as the old shack groaned in the wind. Who had Frederick been in life? What torments had he meted out or endured that made him now so restless when she, Nancy, had never felt so at peace? Had he died inside one of his precious cars, a grisly collision on a moonlit country highway, his leg trapped beneath the buckled hood? Had he been driving? Had he died alone? Nancy's imagination spiraled. It was the same sort of poisonous wonder that once led her to brood over the lives of the children who'd bullied her boys at school. She used to sit in her rocking chair late at night after Lewis had gone to bed, picturing every detail: their stubby fingers and crooked teeth, the snapped pencils and bits of thread and cracker crumbs jammed in their pockets, the bed hair they woke with each morning, the mothers who cradled them as infants—how impossible it was to conceive of ill intent within that bundled warmth.

One day, Nancy floated down to the ravaged sedan where the ghost was resting.

"If we're gonna live here together, we may as well be civil about it." She stuck out her hand. "My name's Nancy. I was born in Wapato in 1935. I died in Seattle. Heart failure."

The ghost stared at her. There was a slackness to his gaze she hadn't noticed before. His nostrils flared, though of course he wasn't taking in any air. "What're you doing here?" he croaked. "You can't stay. Get out." The words lacked any menace. It was almost as though he were speaking to himself. He clawed for the garbage piled in the passenger seat. "Goddammit, Frederick. Goddammit." He reached and reached, but his fingers passed right through it.

Time functioned differently in the world of ghosts. The sun lifted and settled. The moon's face flickered as clouds twisted past like gray rags wrung in slow motion. Seasons changed. It had been the height of summer when Nancy died; now the long blue afternoons shorted out into dusk a little sooner each day. Leaves fell, gathered, and wheeled in orange eddies. Frost thickened on the windowpanes, neither warm nor cold against Nancy's fingers. She observed all this. She knew time was passing, but she didn't feel the itch of it behind her eyeballs. She was, somehow, outside of time. Ten minutes didn't feel so different from a week. A week was a year. One year could be five.

So it took her a while to notice Frederick was gone, and when she had, she couldn't be sure whether he'd been absent a few days or far longer. She floated through the rotted ceiling and onto the roof. The night was cold and clear and full of starlight. Farmland stretched in every direction, gleaming under fresh snow. In the distance, the bulb of the water tower hovered over the city's small cluster of lights. Ghosts would be drawn to the thing's lofty mystique like lost ships to a lighthouse. Was it to the water tower that Frederick had fled? Or was he traveling farther—drifting west across the state until he hit ocean, until his body paled and his thoughts shrank and he was just a lost fragment spinning in that salty vastness? It was his own fault. He would rather fade than share space with her, and so he had gone, and wasn't this how it should be? Nancy thought of how different her life might have turned out, and the lives of her parents, if the people who'd feared and detested them had taken it upon themselves to vanish.

She glided to the floor. Until now, she'd performed her aerial stunts up by the rafters and hadn't spent much time down here. Now she counted the old markers of domesticity she had missed: scraps of wallpaper drooping at the baseboards, a scarred divot where the stove had been pried out, a fistful of wires dangling from a chasm in the wall, the splintered wreckage of some bureau or wardrobe that had been overlooked when the final tenants moved away—all of this lurking around and among Frederick's cars, fossilized remnants of an earlier time.

But it was the door that really held her attention. The kicked-in door, still faintly blue beneath grime and mold, lying on the floor where it had landed when the first trespasser—some farmer's boy on a dare—forced his way inside the empty house. And what fear would've seized him at the sight of the ruined hall, the shadows flailing in the sudden light streaming through the doorway. He would feign indifference for his friends, but he would know then the particular dread of the abandoned home, the stories held between the walls like bated breath.

Nancy squatted with her back to the night and worked her fingers beneath the rotting wood. The door weighed a ton. She strained and shoved. Though all the aches of life had left her, she was no stronger now than she'd ever been. She looked over her shoulder, hoping for the glare of some approaching luminescence. Lewis, arms thrown wide in greeting. Or her parents: her mother laughing at this strange reclamation, her father pinching the skin on his neck—a nervous habit he'd developed after Minidoka—like he couldn't believe, even now, that a home should open itself to them so easily.

The wind scraped its way through the bare, bony trees. Long strips of loose siding fluttered and smacked the shack's walls. There was no one. But it was all right. Nancy returned to the rooftop and rested against the crumbling chimney. She had plenty of time, and a good place to wait.

ACKNOWLEDGEMENTS

I want to gratefully acknowledge the editors of the following publications where the stories listed first appeared, sometimes in alternate forms:

"Princess Shipwreck" in *SmokeLong Quarterly*; "Biohack" in *Joyland*; "The Line" in *Burrow Press Review*; "The Runaway Restaurant" in *The Normal School*; "Night Shift" in *The Cincinnati Review*; "Others Like You" in *Hayden's Ferry Review*; "Preservation" in *Wigleaf*; "What Do You Dream?" in *PRISM International*; "Runners" in *The Cossack Review*; "Wonder in Her Wake" in *Southern Indiana Review*; and "Haunting Grounds" in *The Carolina Quarterly*.

I have benefited from the guidance and inspiration of many different people and groups along the way. Special thanks are due to:

The teachers who got me started and kept me going, especially Paul Graham, Stephanie Elizondo Griest, Pedro Ponce, Maura Stanton, George Steele, and Samrat Upadhyay.

The Indiana University MFA program, where the earliest stories included here were drafted, and my Wild Writing Group— Lauren, Yume, Nicholas, and Sameem—who provided feedback and encouragement as I wrote and revised the last ones.

The Martha's Vineyard Institute of Creative Writing and the Tin

House Summer Workshop. Writing can be lonely work, but communities like these make it less so.

Leland Cheuk, without whom this book would not be a book. Thank you for making me a part of the 7.13 Books family, and for all you do for debut fiction authors.

Finally, to my parents: Thank you for never trying to coerce me into medical school. Thank you for never doubting.

ABOUT THE AUTHOR

Tessa Yang's stories have appeared in *The Cincinnati Review*, *Joyland*, *Foglifter*, and elsewhere. Her flash fiction was included in *Wigleaf's* Top 50 Very Short Fictions of 2018 and 2019. She received her MFA from Indiana University and currently lives in upstate New York, where she teaches creative writing at Hartwick College and is at work on a novel. *The Runaway Restaurant* is her debut collection. Find her online at www.tessayang.com, or follow her on Twitter: @ThePtessadactyl.